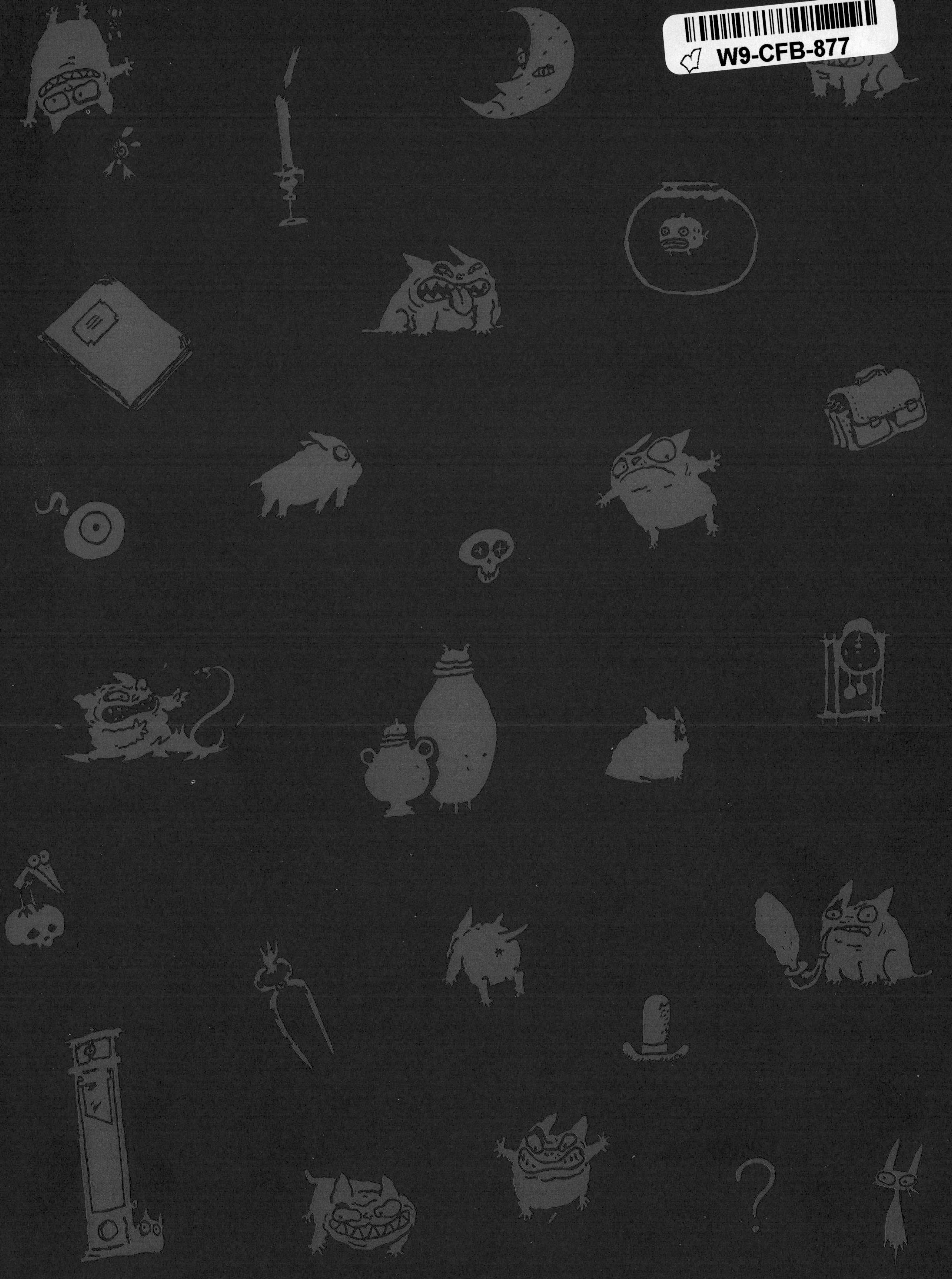

LITTLE VAMPIRE

DOES KUNG FU!

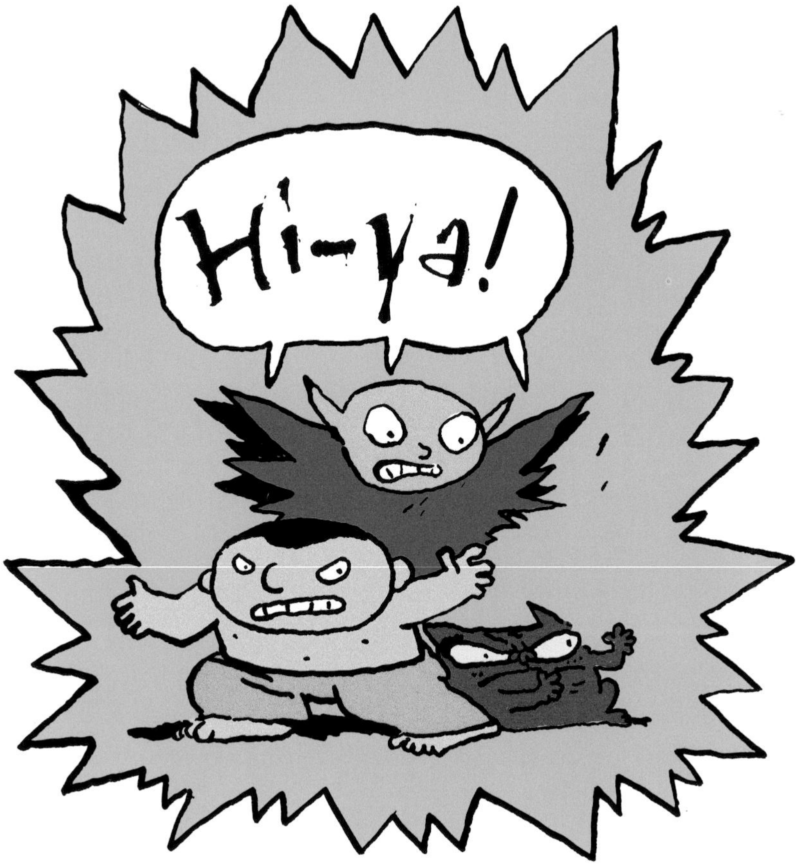
Hi-ya!

Stories and drawings by
Joann Sfar

Colors by
Walter

Simon & Schuster Books for Young Readers
New York London Toronto Sydney Singapore

SIMON & SCHUSTER BOOKS FOR YOUNG READERS
An imprint of Simon & Schuster Children's Publishing Division
1230 Avenue of the Americas, New York, New York 10020

Originally published in France in 2000 as *Petit Vampire fait du Kung-Fu !* by Guy Delcourt
Productions

Translated by Mark and Alexis Siegel
Book design by Mark Siegel
The text for this book is set in Printhouse and Wendy.
The illustrations for this book are rendered in ink and digital color.

Manufactured in France
10 9 8 7 6 5 4 3 2 1
CIP data for this book is available from the Library of Congress.
ISBN 0-689-85769-1

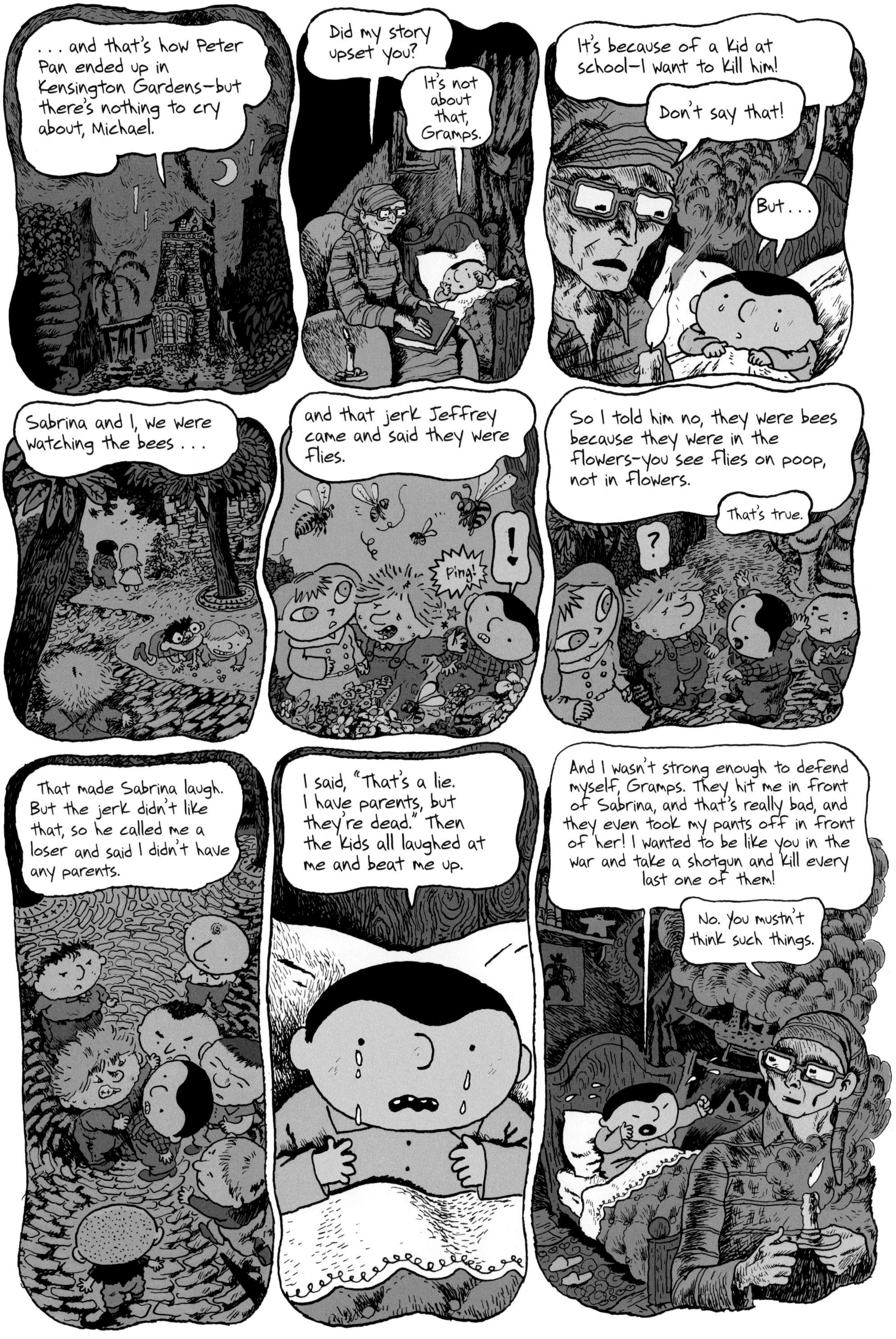

. . . and that's how Peter Pan ended up in Kensington Gardens—but there's nothing to cry about, Michael.
Did my story upset you?
It's not about that, Gramps.
It's because of a kid at school—I want to kill him!
Don't say that!
But . . .
Sabrina and I, we were watching the bees . . .
and that jerk Jeffrey came and said they were flies.
Ping!
!
So I told him no, they were bees because they were in the flowers—you see flies on poop, not in flowers.
That's true.
?
That made Sabrina laugh. But the jerk didn't like that, so he called me a loser and said I didn't have any parents.
I said, "That's a lie. I have parents, but they're dead." Then the kids all laughed at me and beat me up.
And I wasn't strong enough to defend myself, Gramps. They hit me in front of Sabrina, and that's really bad, and they even took my pants off in front of her! I wanted to be like you in the war and take a shotgun and kill every last one of them!
No. You mustn't think such things.

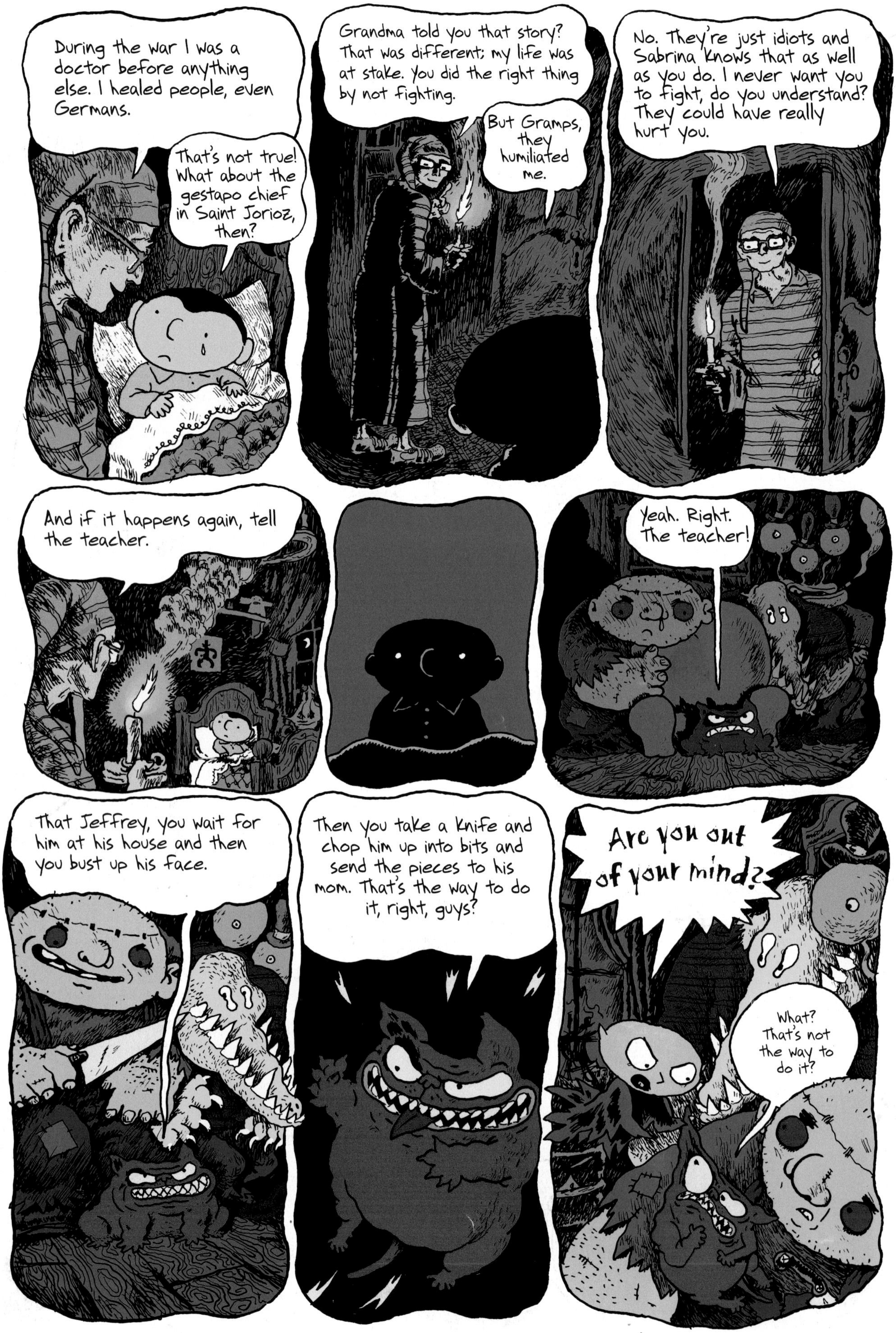
During the war I was a doctor before anything else. I healed people, even Germans.
That's not true! What about the gestapo chief in Saint Jorioz, then?
Grandma told you that story? That was different; my life was at stake. You did the right thing by not fighting.
But Gramps, they humiliated me.
No. They're just idiots and Sabrina knows that as well as you do. I never want you to fight, do you understand? They could have really hurt you.
And if it happens again, tell the teacher.
Yeah. Right. The teacher!
That Jeffrey, you wait for him at his house and then you bust up his face.
Then you take a knife and chop him up into bits and send the pieces to his mom. That's the way to do it, right, guys?
Are you out of your mind?
What? That's not the way to do it?

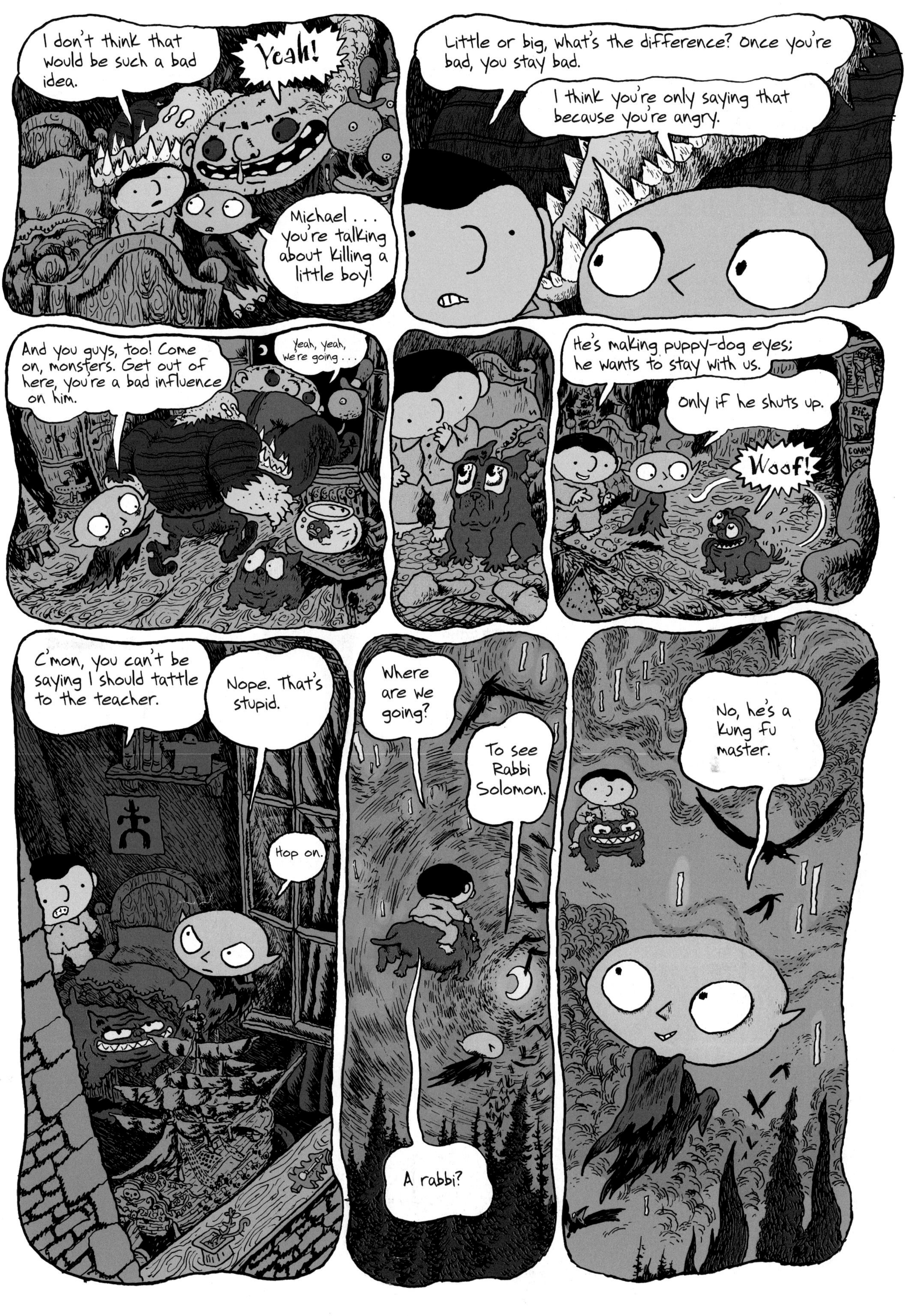
I don't think that would be such a bad idea.
Yeah!
Michael . . . you're talking about killing a little boy!
Little or big, what's the difference? Once you're bad, you stay bad.
I think you're only saying that because you're angry.
And you guys, too! Come on, monsters. Get out of here, you're a bad influence on him.
Yeah, yeah, we're going . . .
He's making puppy-dog eyes; he wants to stay with us.
Only if he shuts up.
Woof!
C'mon, you can't be saying I should tattle to the teacher.
Nope. That's stupid.
Hop on.
Where are we going?
To see Rabbi Solomon.
A rabbi?
No, he's a kung fu master.

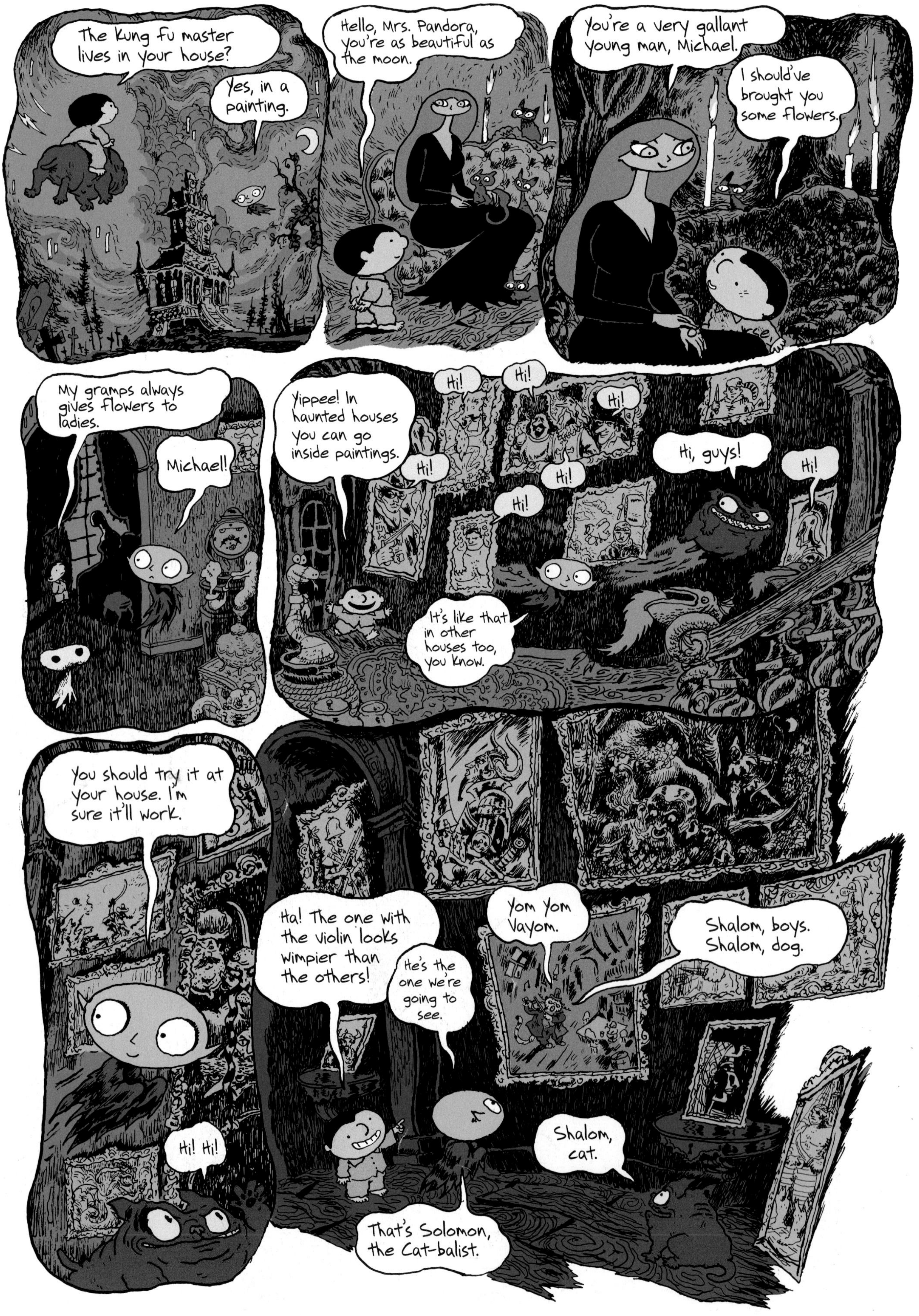

The kung fu master lives in your house?
Yes, in a painting.
Hello, Mrs. Pandora, you're as beautiful as the moon.
You're a very gallant young man, Michael.
I should've brought you some flowers.
My gramps always gives flowers to ladies.
Michael!
Yippee! In haunted houses you can go inside paintings.
Hi!
Hi!
Hi!
Hi!
Hi!
Hi!
Hi, guys!
Hi!
It's like that in other houses too, you know.
You should try it at your house. I'm sure it'll work.
Hi! Hi!
Ha! The one with the violin looks wimpier than the others!
He's the one we're going to see.
Yom Yom Vayom.
Shalom, boys. Shalom, dog.
Shalom, cat.
That's Solomon, the Cat-balist.

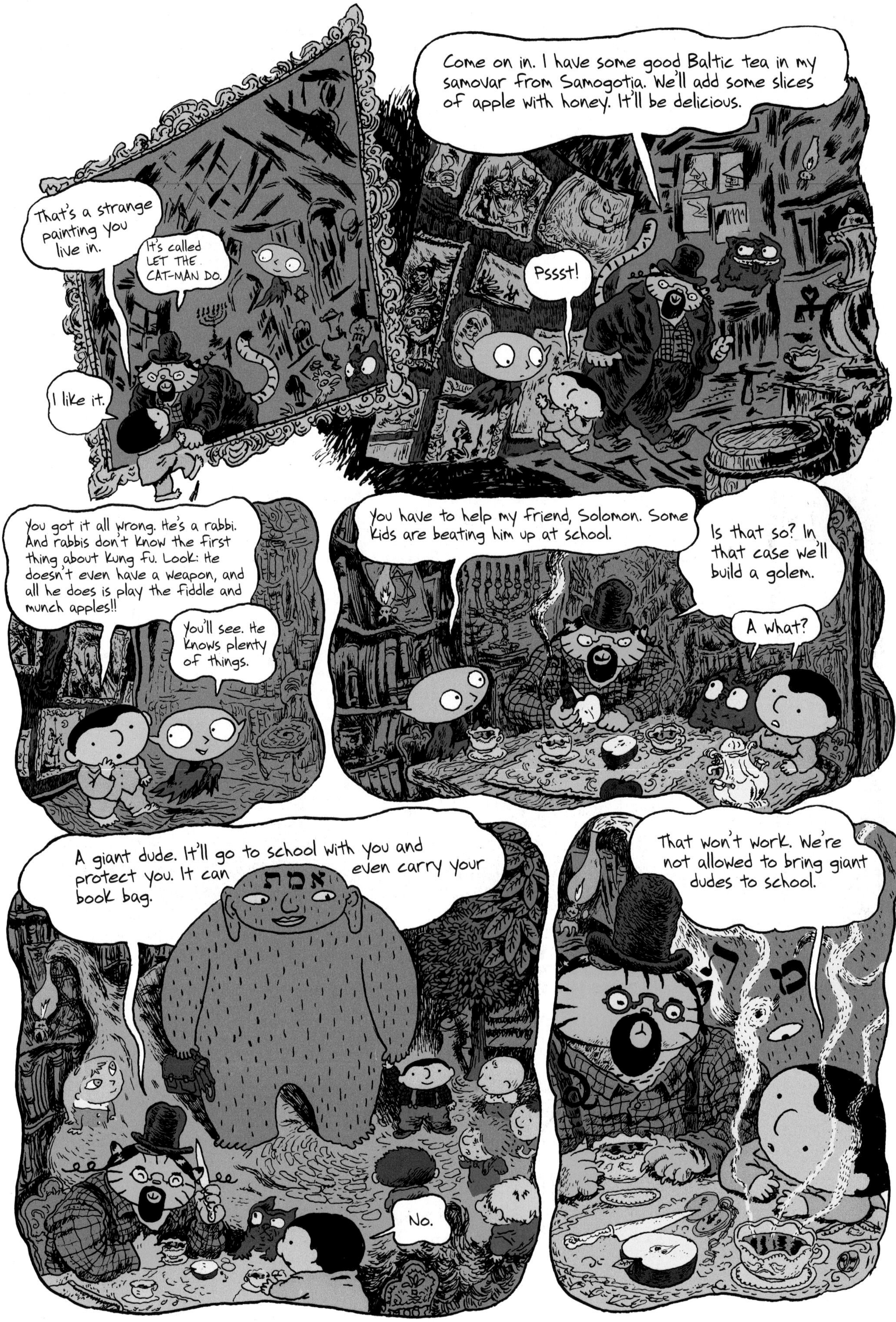
That's a strange painting you live in.
It's called LET THE CAT-MAN DO.
I like it.
Come on in. I have some good Baltic tea in my samovar from Samogotia. We'll add some slices of apple with honey. It'll be delicious.
Pssst!
You got it all wrong. He's a rabbi. And rabbis don't know the first thing about kung fu. Look: He doesn't even have a weapon, and all he does is play the fiddle and munch apples!!
You'll see. He knows plenty of things.
You have to help my friend, Solomon. Some kids are beating him up at school.
Is that so? In that case we'll build a golem.
A what?
A giant dude. It'll go to school with you and protect you. It can even carry your book bag.
אמת
No.
That won't work. We're not allowed to bring giant dudes to school.

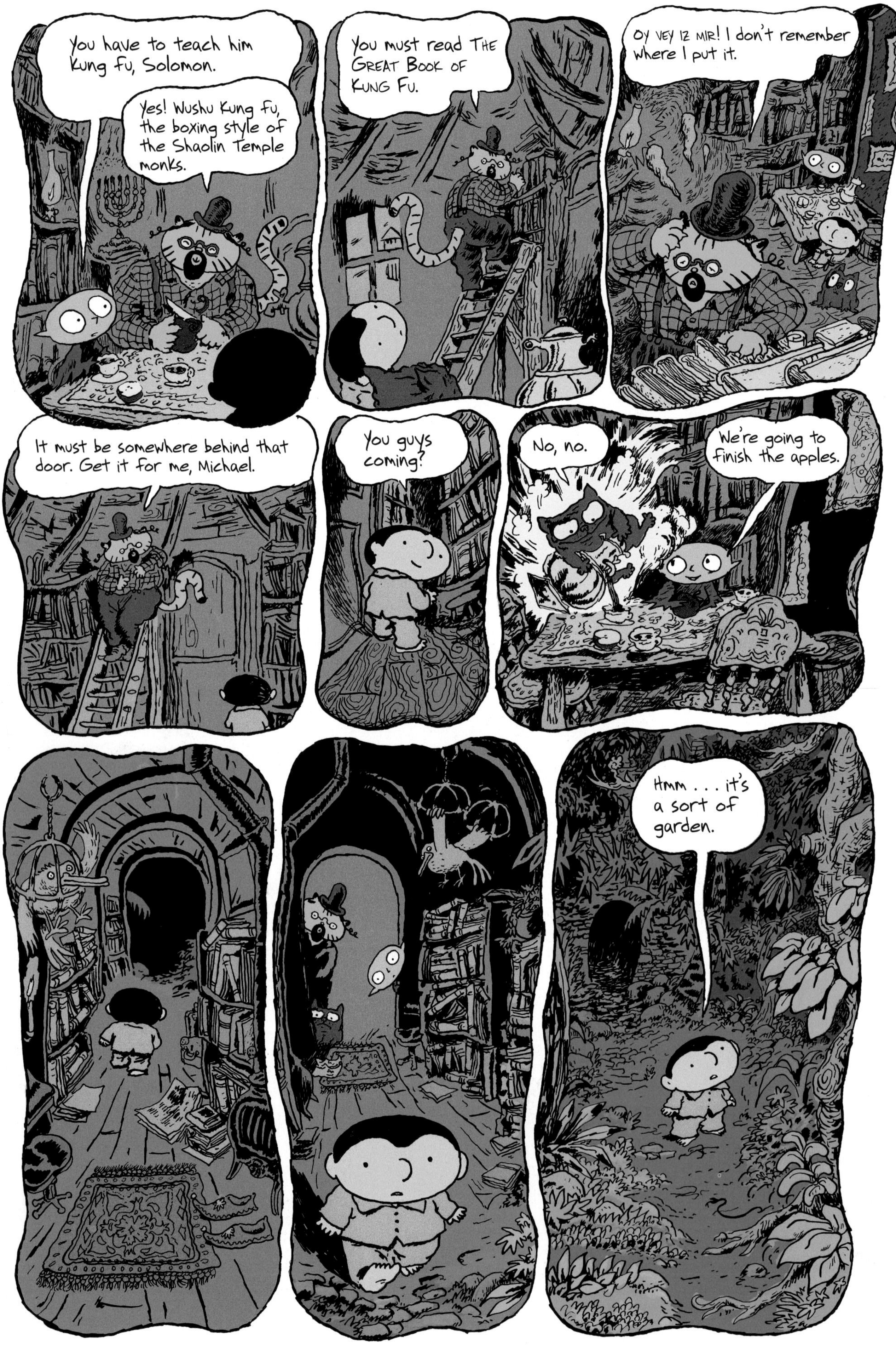
You have to teach him Kung Fu, Solomon.
Yes! Wushu Kung Fu, the boxing style of the Shaolin Temple monks.
You must read THE GREAT BOOK OF KUNG FU.
OY VEY IZ MIR! I don't remember where I put it.
It must be somewhere behind that door. Get it for me, Michael.
You guys coming?
No, no.
We're going to finish the apples.
Hmm . . . it's a sort of garden.

What a strange place to forget a book!

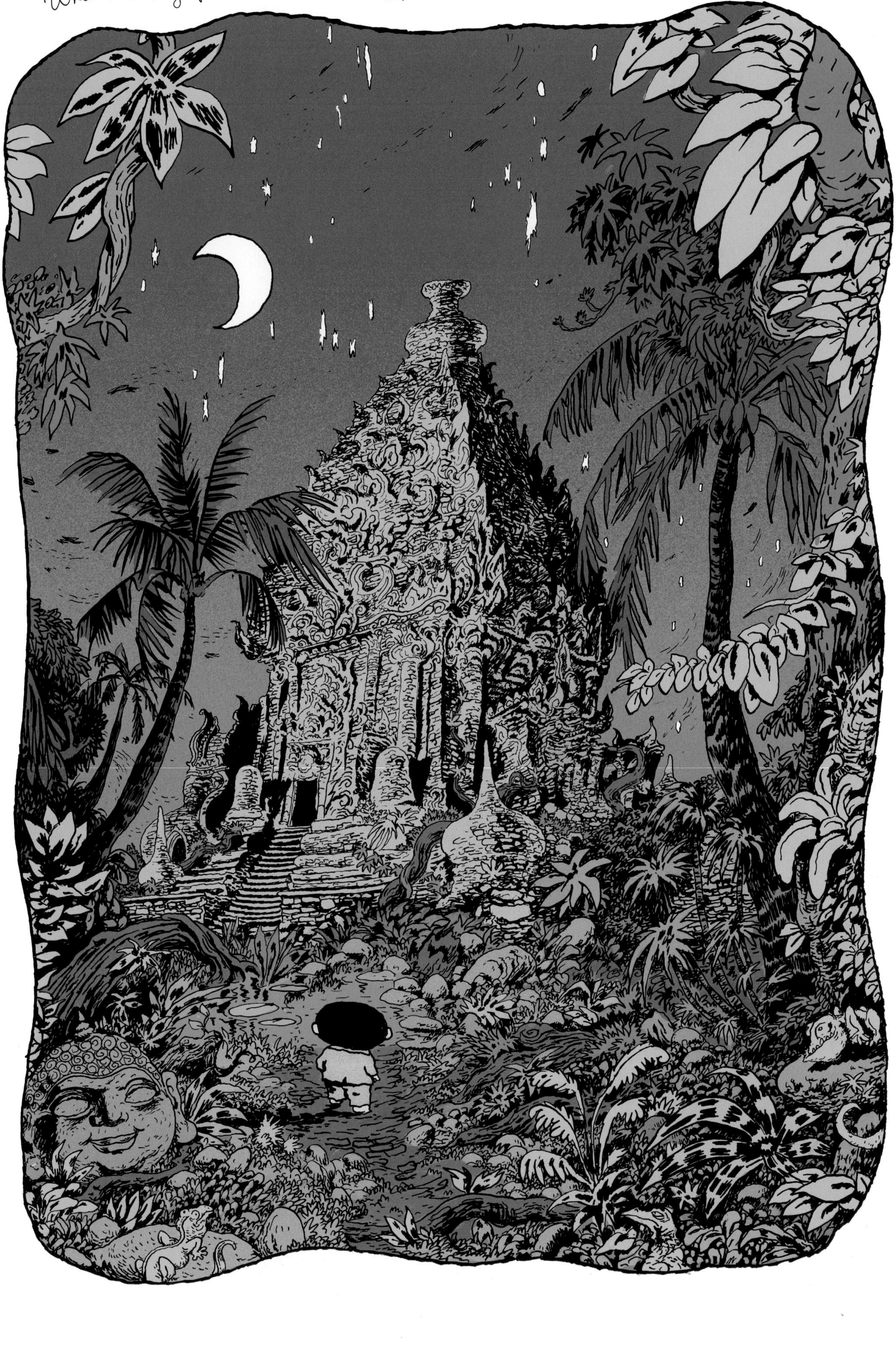

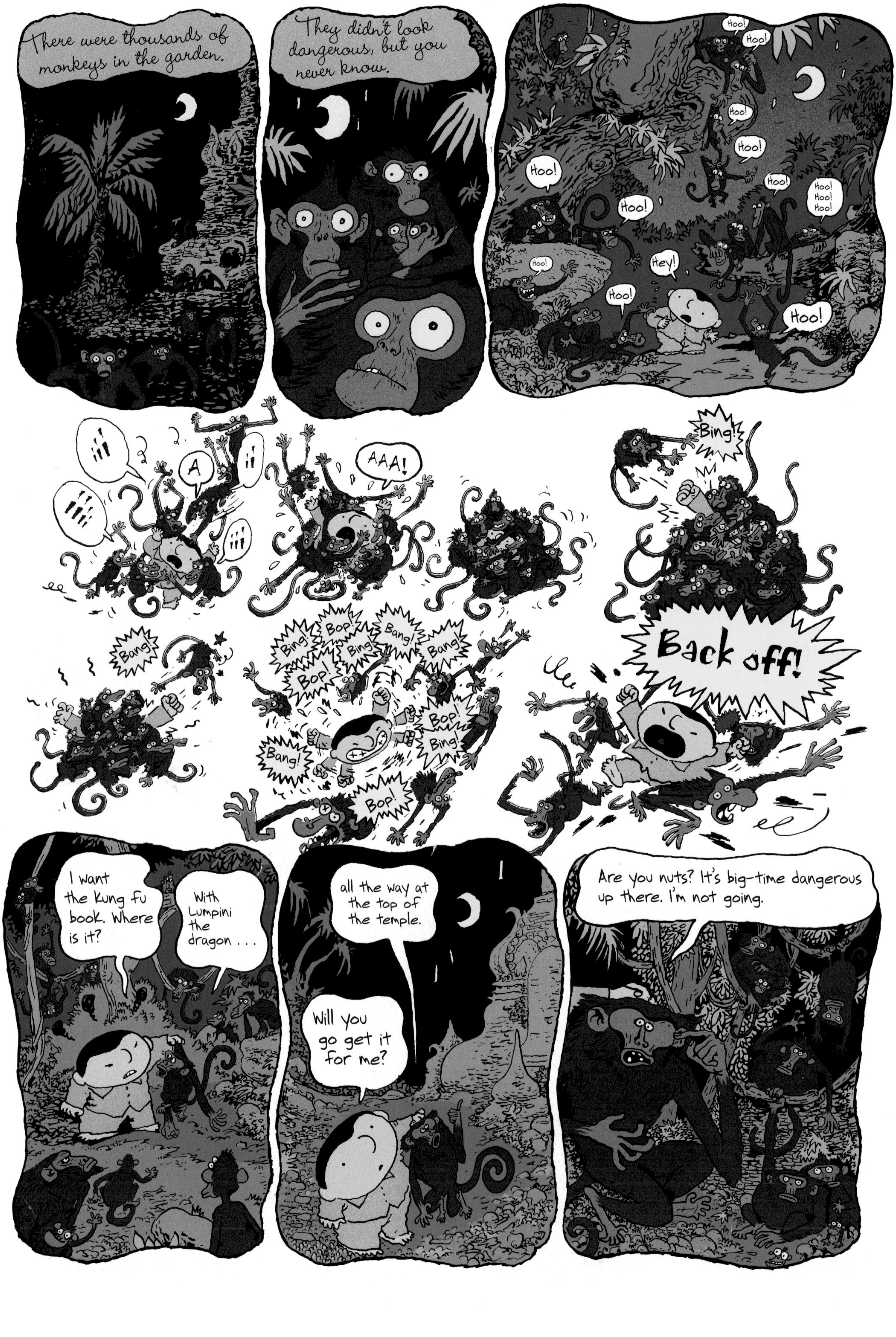
There were thousands of monkeys in the garden.
They didn't look dangerous, but you never know.
Hoo!
Hoo!
Hoo!
Hoo!
Hoo!
Hoo!
Hoo! Hoo! Hoo!
Hoo!
Hoo!
Hey!
Hoo!
Hoo!
A
AAA!
Bing!
Bang!
Bing!
Bop!
Bang!
Bing!
Bang!
Bop!
Bop!
Bing!
Bang!
Bop!
Back off!
I want the Kung fu book. Where is it?
With Lumpini the dragon . . .
all the way at the top of the temple.
Will you go get it for me?
Are you nuts? It's big-time dangerous up there. I'm not going.

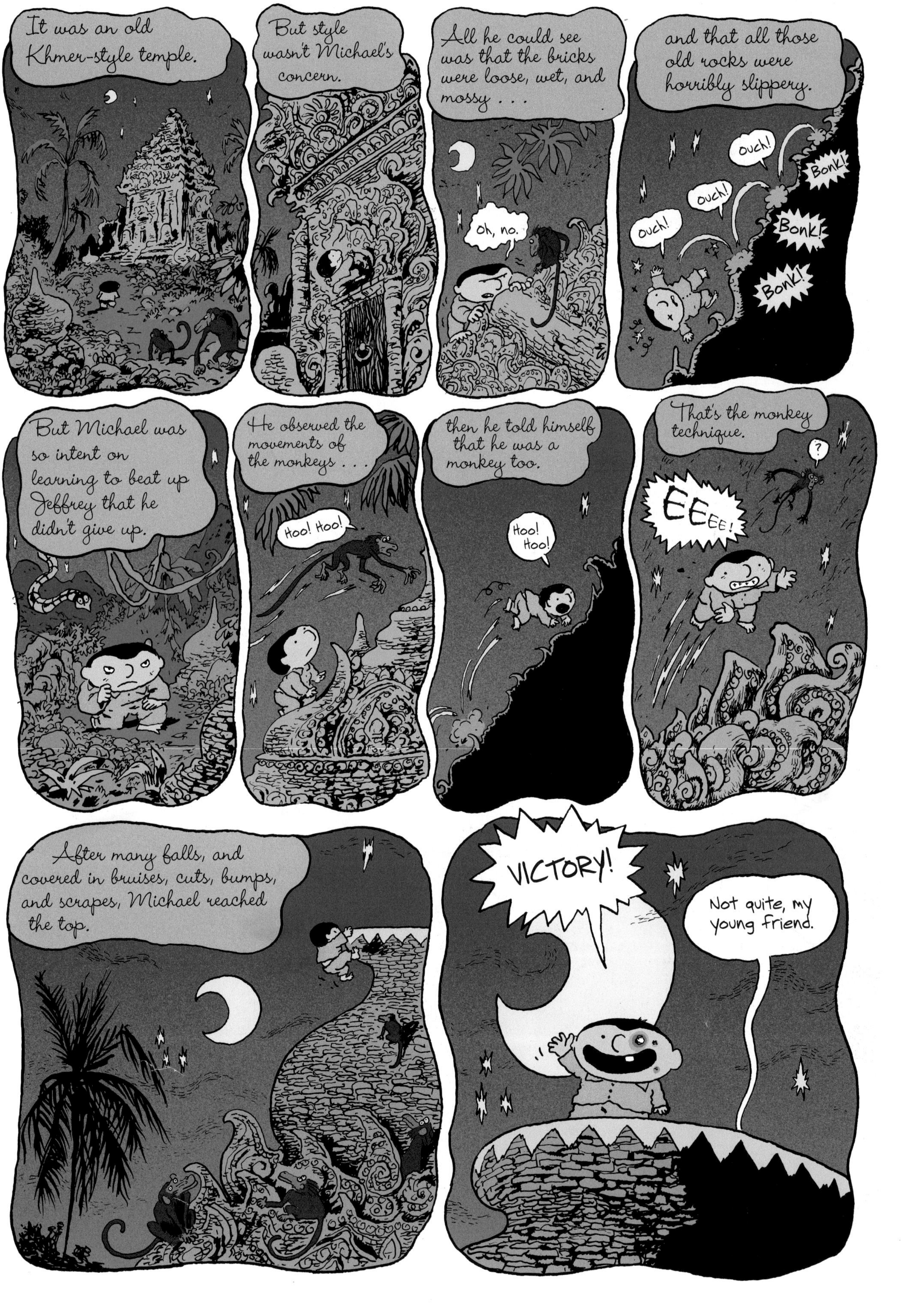

It was an old Khmer-style temple.
But style wasn't Michael's concern.
All he could see was that the bricks were loose, wet, and mossy . . .
Oh, no.
and that all those old rocks were horribly slippery.
Ouch!
Ouch!
Ouch!
Bonk!
Bonk!
Bonk!
But Michael was so intent on learning to beat up Jeffrey that he didn't give up.
He observed the movements of the monkeys . . .
Hoo! Hoo!
then he told himself that he was a monkey too.
Hoo! Hoo!
That's the monkey technique.
?
EEEEE!
After many falls, and covered in bruises, cuts, bumps, and scrapes, Michael reached the top.
VICTORY!
Not quite, my young friend.

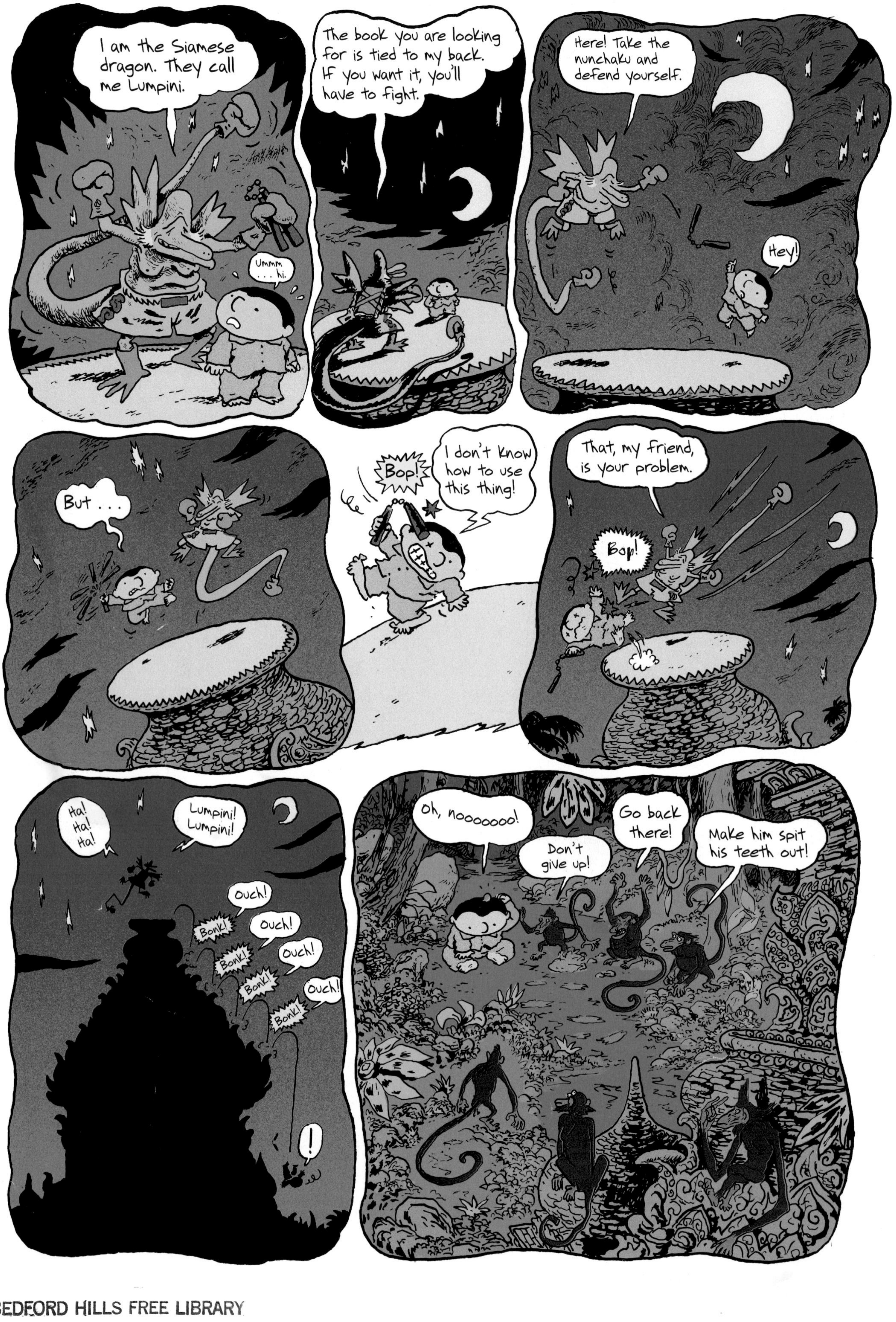
I am the Siamese dragon. They call me Lumpini.
Ummm . . . hi.
The book you are looking for is tied to my back. If you want it, you'll have to fight.
Here! Take the nunchaku and defend yourself.
Hey!
But . . .
Bop!
I don't know how to use this thing!
That, my friend, is your problem.
Bop!
Ha! Ha! Ha!
Lumpini! Lumpini!
Ouch!
Bonk!
Ouch!
Bonk!
Ouch!
Bonk!
Ouch!
Bonk!
!
Oh, noooooooo!
Don't give up!
Go back there!
Make him spit his teeth out!

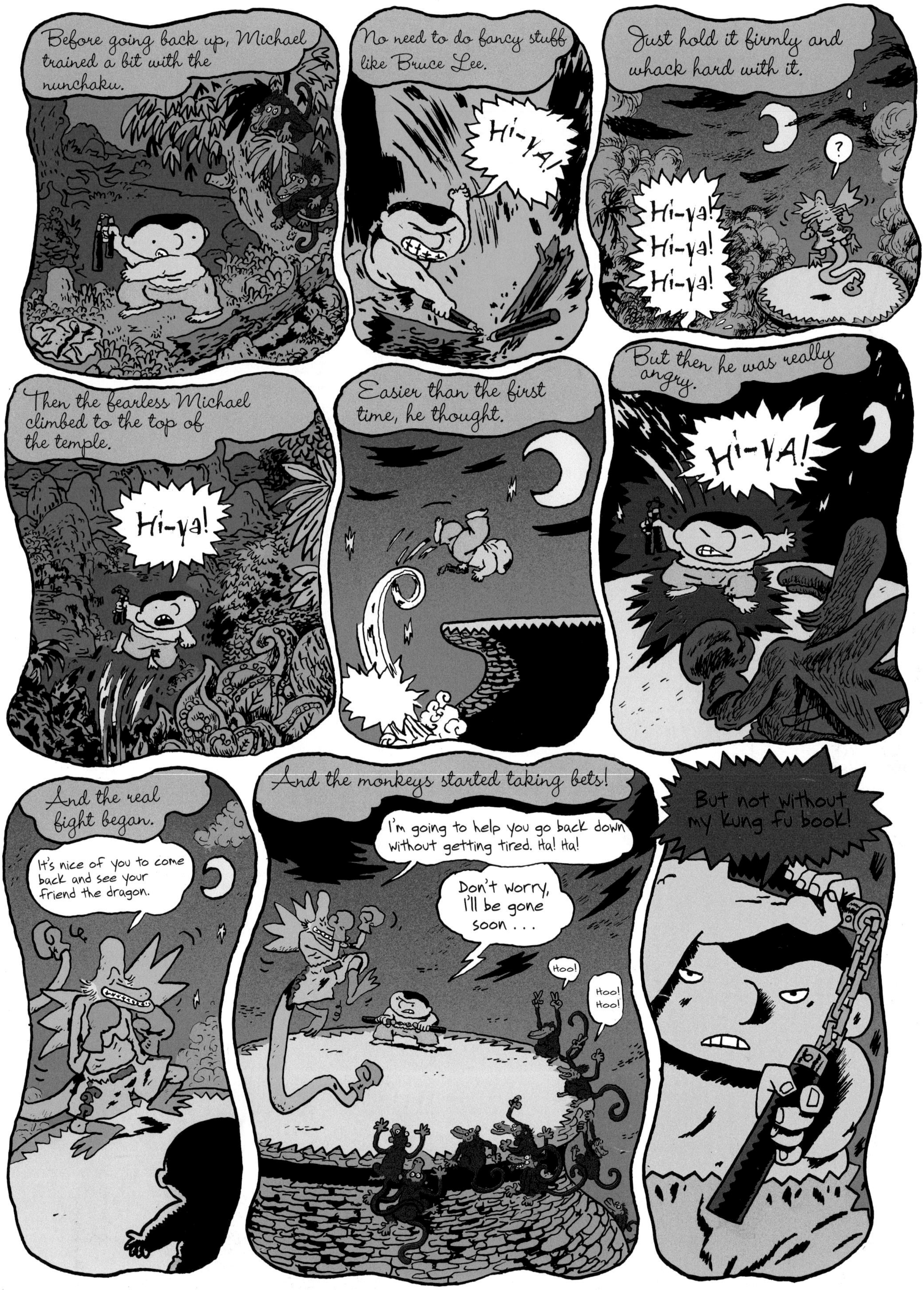
Before going back up, Michael trained a bit with the nunchaku.
No need to do fancy stuff like Bruce Lee.
Hi-YA!
Just hold it firmly and whack hard with it.
Hi-ya! Hi-ya! Hi-ya!
?
Then the fearless Michael climbed to the top of the temple.
Hi-ya!
Easier than the first time, he thought.
But then he was really angry.
Hi-YA!
And the real fight began.
It's nice of you to come back and see your friend the dragon.
And the monkeys started taking bets!
I'm going to help you go back down without getting tired. Ha! Ha!
Don't worry, I'll be gone soon . . .
Hoo!
Hoo! Hoo!
But not without my kung fu book!

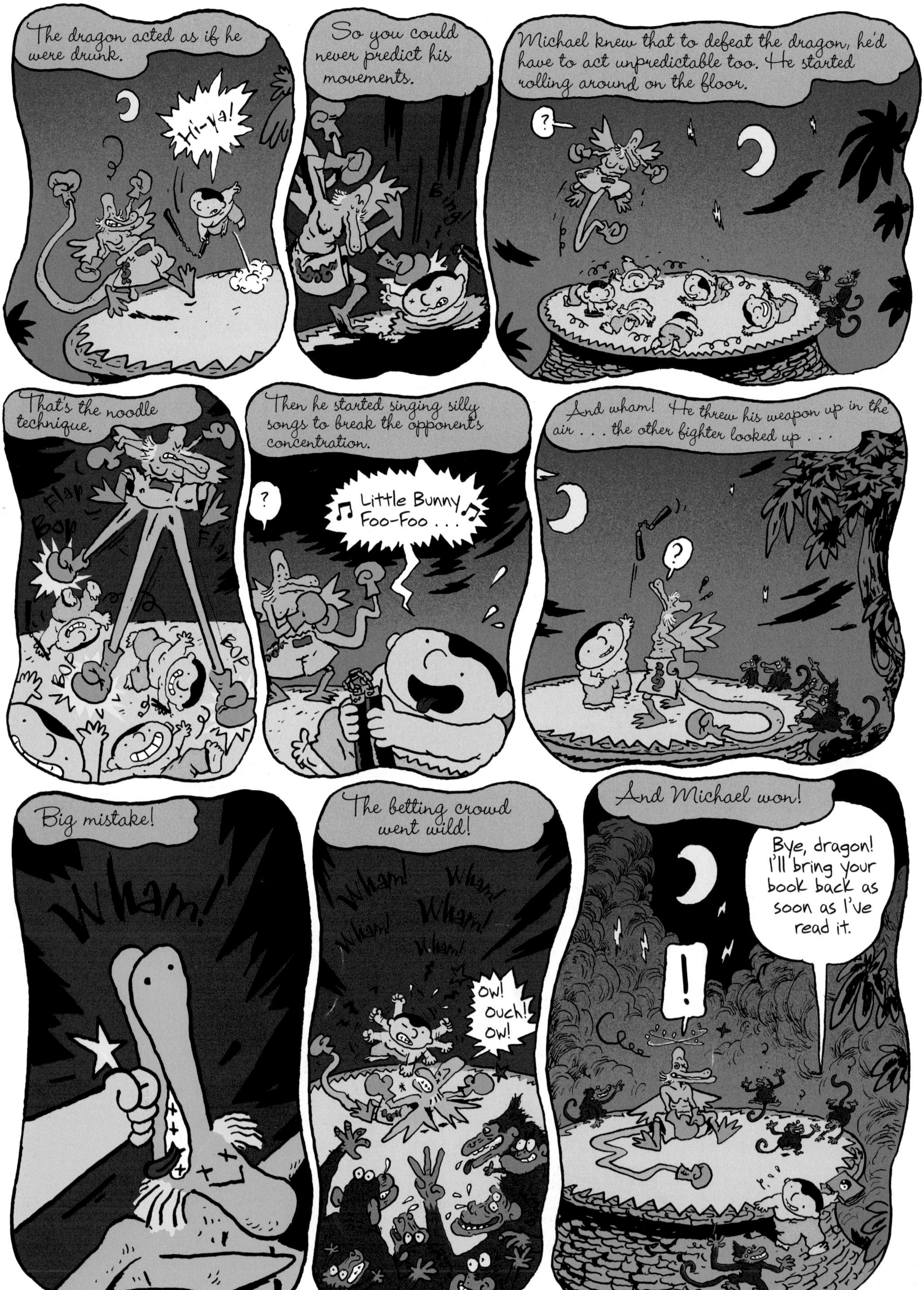

The dragon acted as if he were drunk.
Hi-ya!
So you could never predict his movements.
Bing!
Michael knew that to defeat the dragon, he'd have to act unpredictable too. He started rolling around on the floor.
?
That's the noodle technique.
Flap
Bop
Flap
BOP
BOP
Then he started singing silly songs to break the opponent's concentration.
?
Little Bunny Foo-Foo . . .
And wham! He threw his weapon up in the air . . . the other fighter looked up . . .
?
Big mistake!
Wham!
The betting crowd went wild!
Wham!
Wham!
Wham!
Wham!
Wham!
Ow! Ouch! Ow!
And Michael won!
Bye, dragon! I'll bring your book back as soon as I've read it.
!

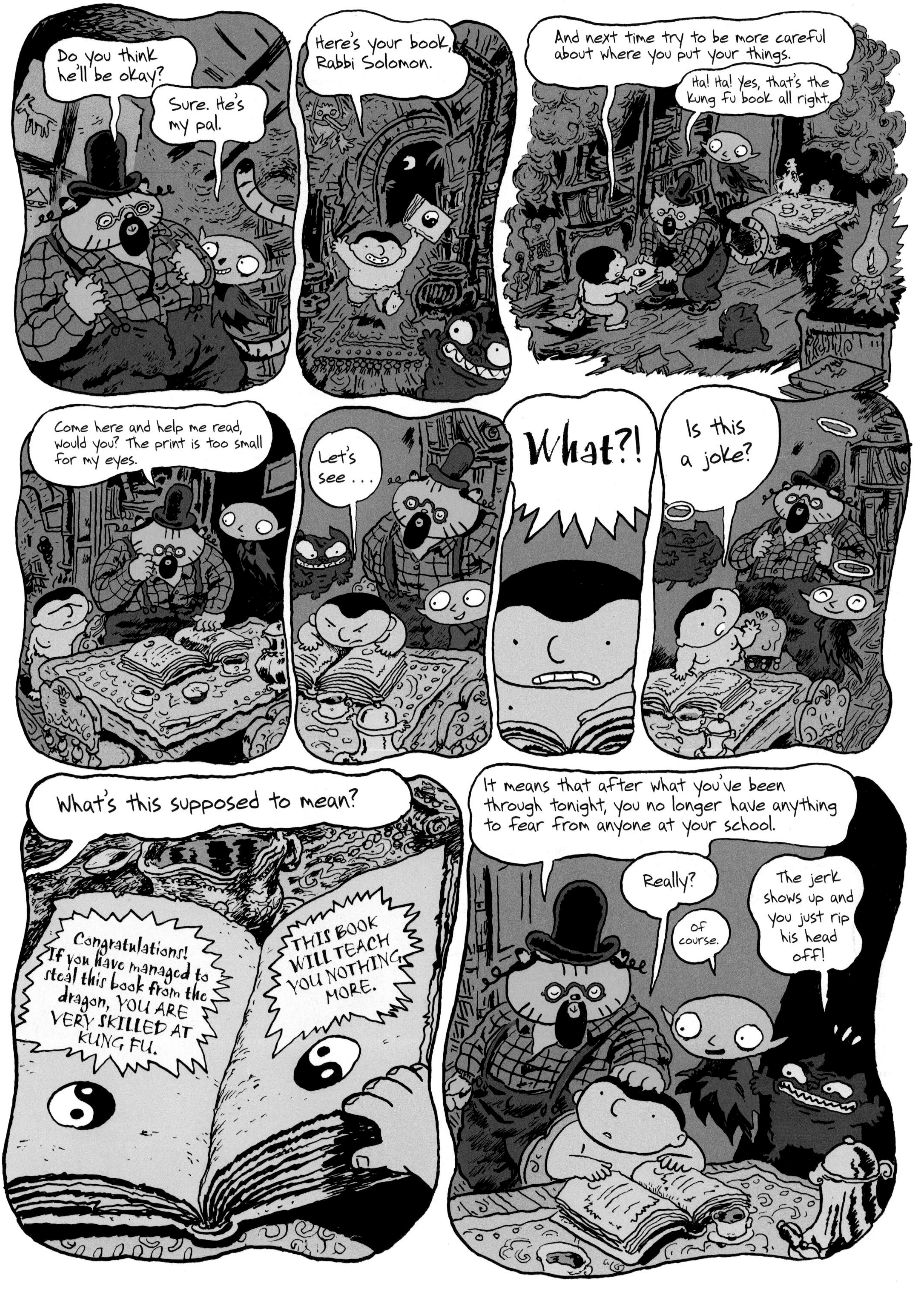
Do you think he'll be okay?
Sure. He's my pal.
Here's your book, Rabbi Solomon.
And next time try to be more careful about where you put your things.
Ha! Ha! Yes, that's the kung fu book all right.
Come here and help me read, would you? The print is too small for my eyes.
Let's see . . .
What?!
Is this a joke?
What's this supposed to mean?
Congratulations! If you have managed to steal this book from the dragon, YOU ARE VERY SKILLED AT KUNG FU.
THIS BOOK WILL TEACH YOU NOTHING MORE.
It means that after what you've been through tonight, you no longer have anything to fear from anyone at your school.
Really?
Of course.
The jerk shows up and you just rip his head off!

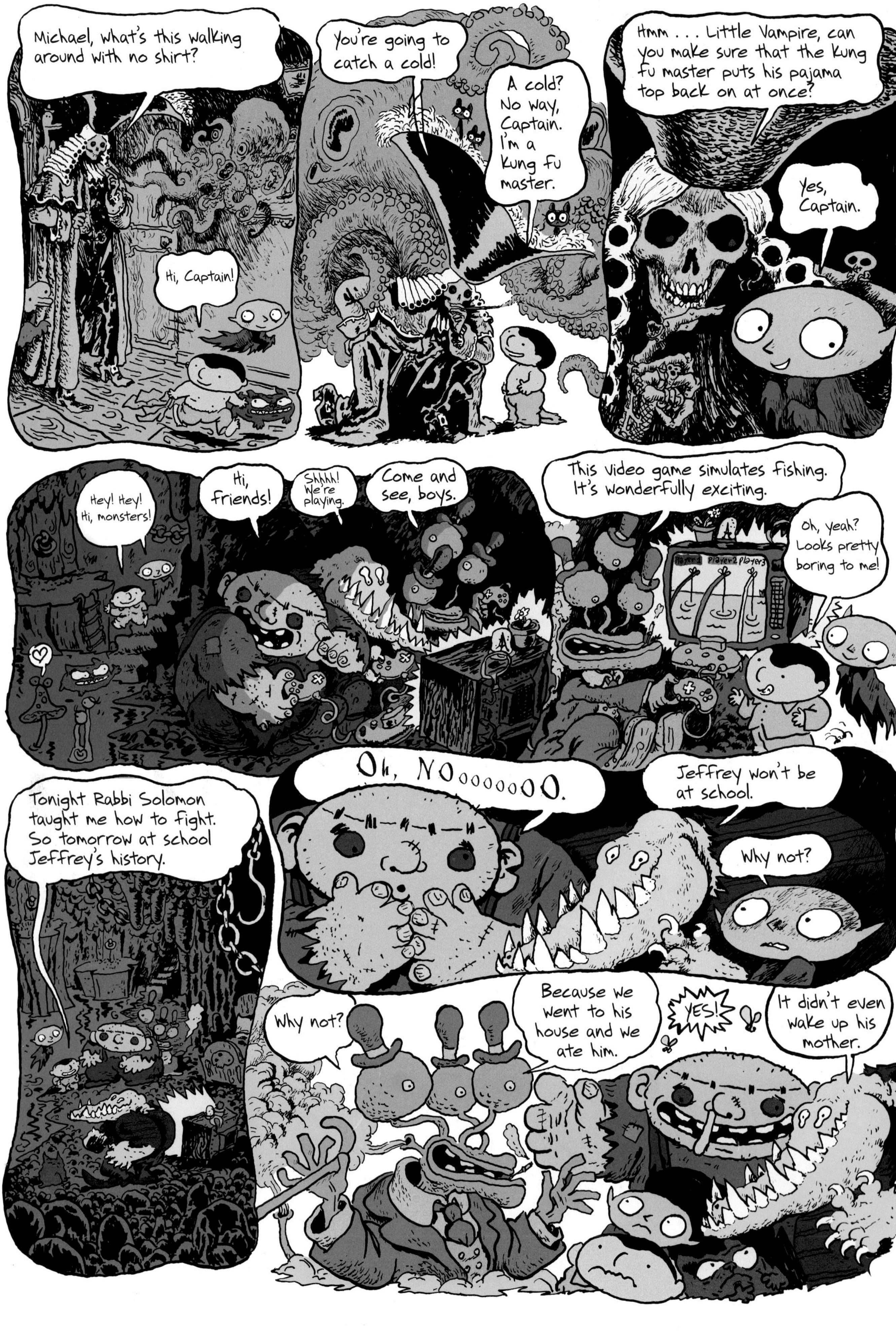
Michael, what's this walking around with no shirt?
Hi, Captain!
You're going to catch a cold!
A cold? No way, Captain. I'm a kung fu master.
Hmm . . . Little Vampire, can you make sure that the kung fu master puts his pajama top back on at once?
Yes, Captain.
Hey! Hey! Hi, monsters!
Hi, friends!
Shhhh! We're playing.
Come and see, boys.
This video game simulates fishing. It's wonderfully exciting.
Oh, yeah? Looks pretty boring to me!
Tonight Rabbi Solomon taught me how to fight. So tomorrow at school Jeffrey's history.
Oh, NOoooooooO.
Jeffrey won't be at school.
Why not?
Why not?
Because we went to his house and we ate him.
YES!
It didn't even wake up his mother.

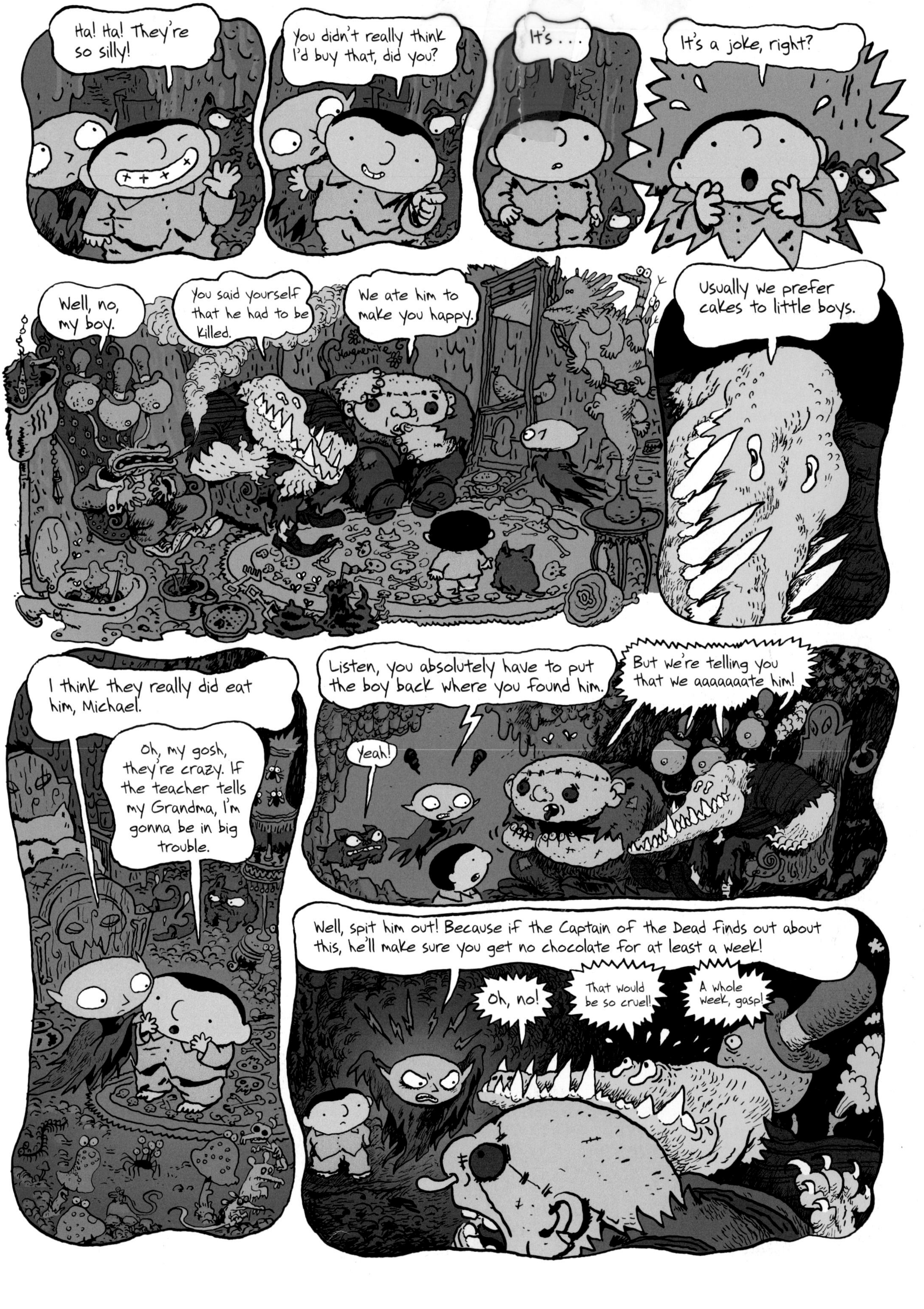

Ha! Ha! They're so silly!
You didn't really think I'd buy that, did you?
It's . . .
It's a joke, right?
Well, no, my boy.
You said yourself that he had to be killed.
We ate him to make you happy.
Usually we prefer cakes to little boys.
I think they really did eat him, Michael.
Oh, my gosh, they're crazy. If the teacher tells my Grandma, I'm gonna be in big trouble.
Listen, you absolutely have to put the boy back where you found him.
Yeah!
But we're telling you that we aaaaaaate him!
Well, spit him out! Because if the Captain of the Dead finds out about this, he'll make sure you get no chocolate for at least a week!
Oh, no!
That would be so cruel!
A whole week, gasp!

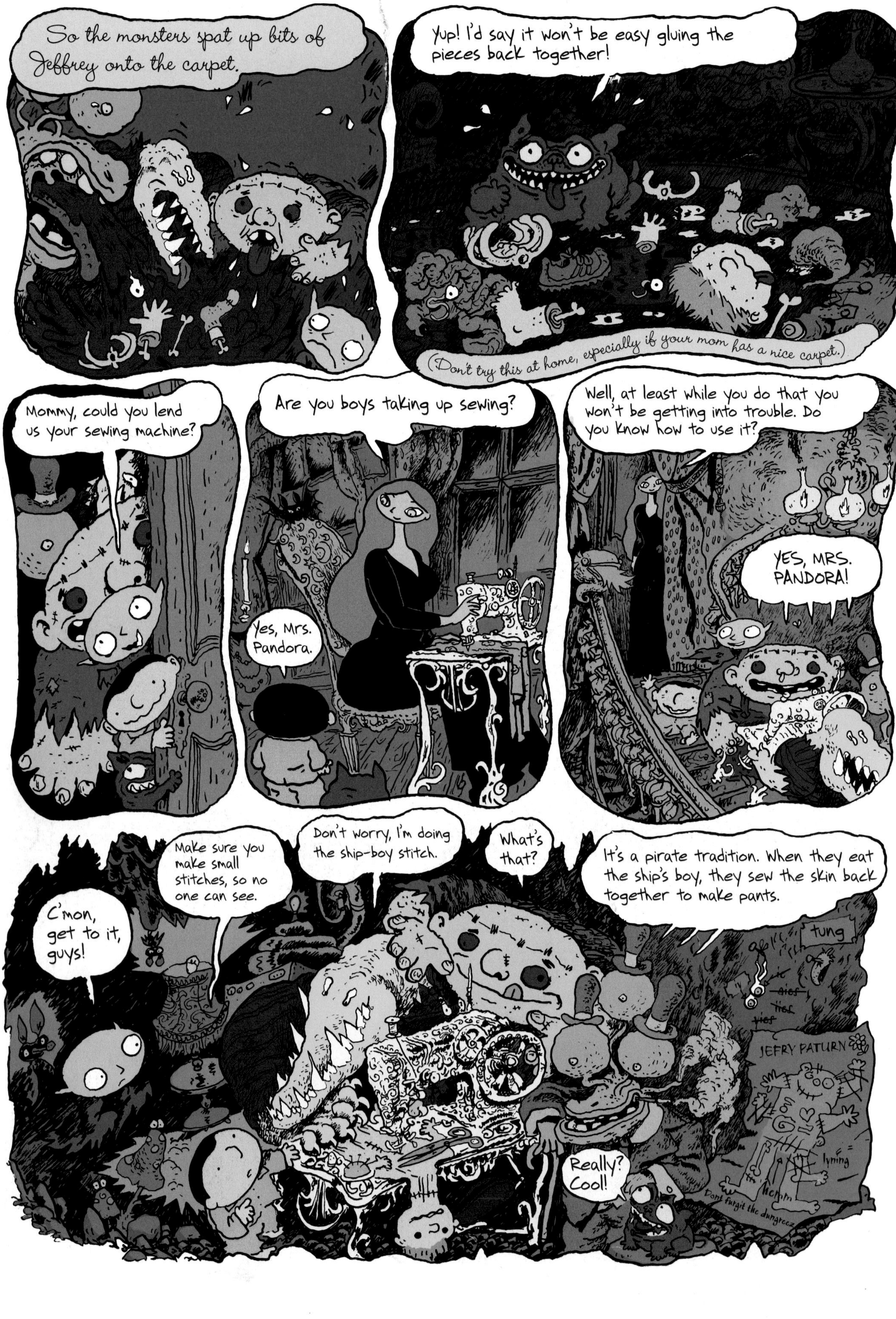
So the monsters spat up bits of Jeffrey onto the carpet.
Yup! I'd say it won't be easy gluing the pieces back together!
(Don't try this at home, especially if your mom has a nice carpet.)
Mommy, could you lend us your sewing machine?
Are you boys taking up sewing?
Yes, Mrs. Pandora.
Well, at least while you do that you won't be getting into trouble. Do you know how to use it?
YES, MRS. PANDORA!
C'mon, get to it, guys!
Make sure you make small stitches, so no one can see.
Don't worry, I'm doing the ship-boy stitch.
What's that?
It's a pirate tradition. When they eat the ship's boy, they sew the skin back together to make pants.
Really? Cool!
tung
JEFRY PATURN
lyning
Dont furgit the dungreez

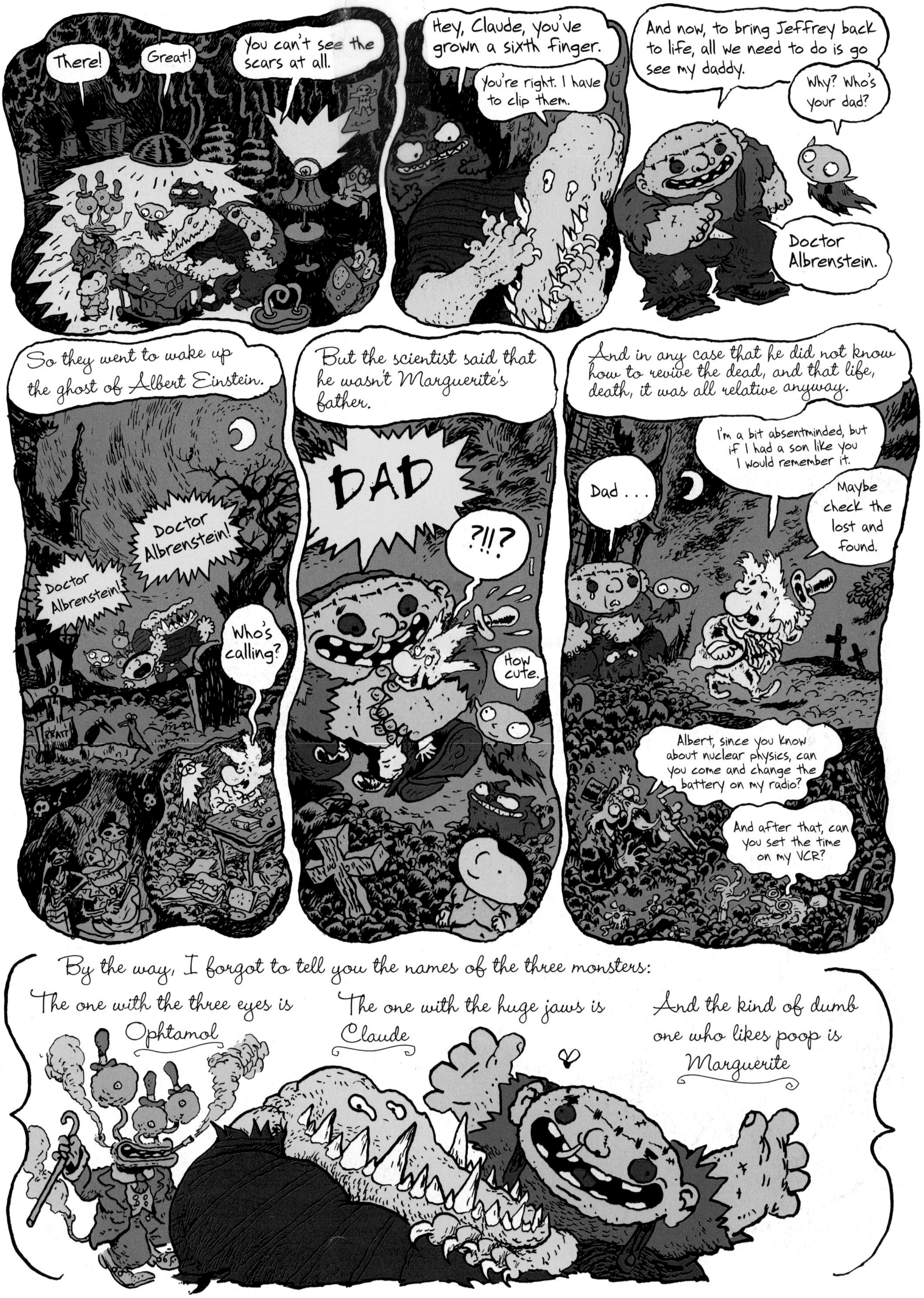
There!
Great!
You can't see the scars at all.
Hey, Claude, you've grown a sixth finger.
You're right. I have to clip them.
And now, to bring Jeffrey back to life, all we need to do is go see my daddy.
Why? Who's your dad?
Doctor Albrenstein.
So they went to wake up the ghost of Albert Einstein.
Doctor Albrenstein!
Doctor Albrenstein!
Who's calling?
But the scientist said that he wasn't Marguerite's father.
DAD
?!!?
How cute.
And in any case that he did not know how to revive the dead, and that life, death, it was all relative anyway.
Dad . . .
I'm a bit absentminded, but if I had a son like you I would remember it.
Maybe check the lost and found.
Albert, since you know about nuclear physics, can you come and change the battery on my radio?
And after that, can you set the time on my VCR?
By the way, I forgot to tell you the names of the three monsters:
The one with the three eyes is Ophtamol
The one with the huge jaws is Claude
And the kind of dumb one who likes poop is Marguerite

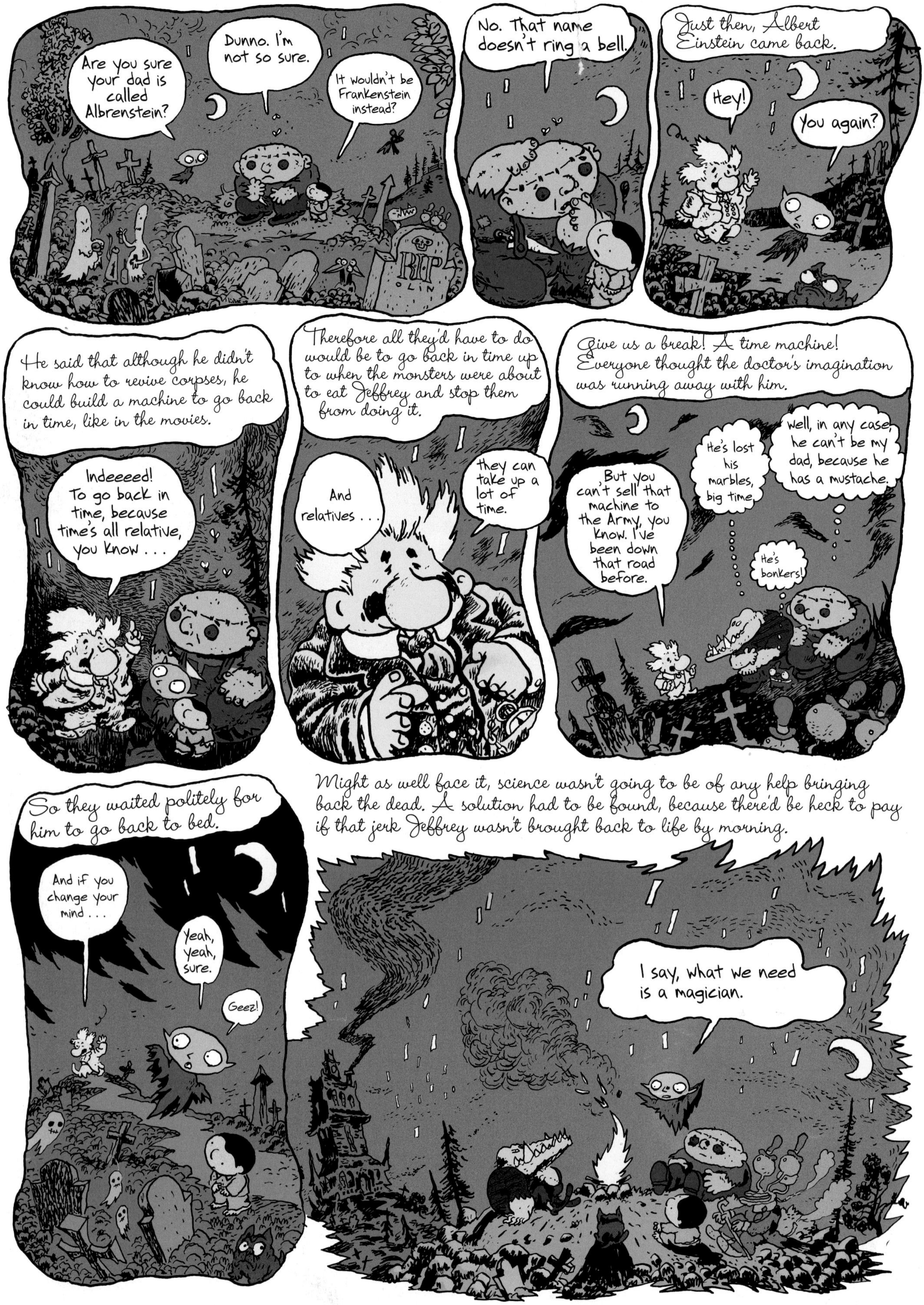
Are you sure your dad is called Albrenstein?
Dunno. I'm not so sure.
It wouldn't be Frankenstein instead?
No. That name doesn't ring a bell.
Just then, Albert Einstein came back.
Hey!
You again?
He said that although he didn't know how to revive corpses, he could build a machine to go back in time, like in the movies.
Indeeeed! To go back in time, because time's all relative, you know . . .
Therefore all they'd have to do would be to go back in time up to when the monsters were about to eat Jeffrey and stop them from doing it.
And relatives . . .
they can take up a lot of time.
Give us a break! A time machine! Everyone thought the doctor's imagination was running away with him.
But you can't sell that machine to the Army, you know. I've been down that road before.
He's lost his marbles, big time.
Well, in any case, he can't be my dad, because he has a mustache.
He's bonkers!
So they waited politely for him to go back to bed.
And if you change your mind . . .
Yeah, yeah, sure.
Geez!
Might as well face it, science wasn't going to be of any help bringing back the dead. A solution had to be found, because there'd be heck to pay if that jerk Jeffrey wasn't brought back to life by morning.
I say, what we need is a magician.

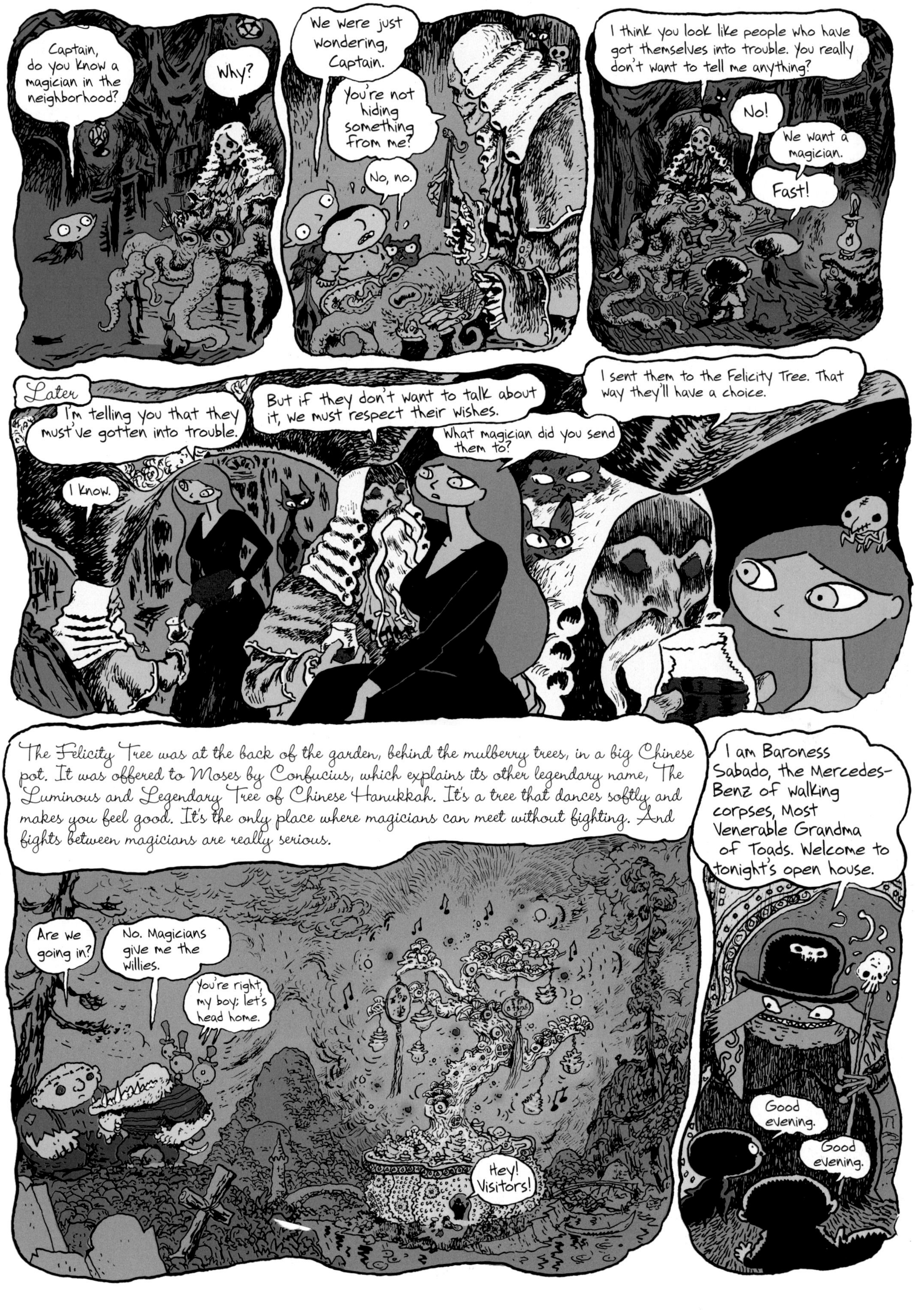

Captain, do you know a magician in the neighborhood?
Why?
We were just wondering, Captain.
You're not hiding something from me?
No, no.
I think you look like people who have got themselves into trouble. You really don't want to tell me anything?
No!
We want a magician.
Fast!
Later
I'm telling you that they must've gotten into trouble.
But if they don't want to talk about it, we must respect their wishes.
I sent them to the Felicity Tree. That way they'll have a choice.
What magician did you send them to?
I know.
The Felicity Tree was at the back of the garden, behind the mulberry trees, in a big Chinese pot. It was offered to Moses by Confucius, which explains its other legendary name, The Luminous and Legendary Tree of Chinese Hanukkah. It's a tree that dances softly and makes you feel good. It's the only place where magicians can meet without fighting. And fights between magicians are really serious.
Are we going in?
No. Magicians give me the willies.
You're right, my boy; let's head home.
Hey! Visitors!
I am Baroness Sabado, the Mercedes-Benz of walking corpses, Most Venerable Grandma of Toads. Welcome to tonight's open house.
Good evening.
Good evening.

They were about to have dinner. Having that many magicians in one place sure was convenient.

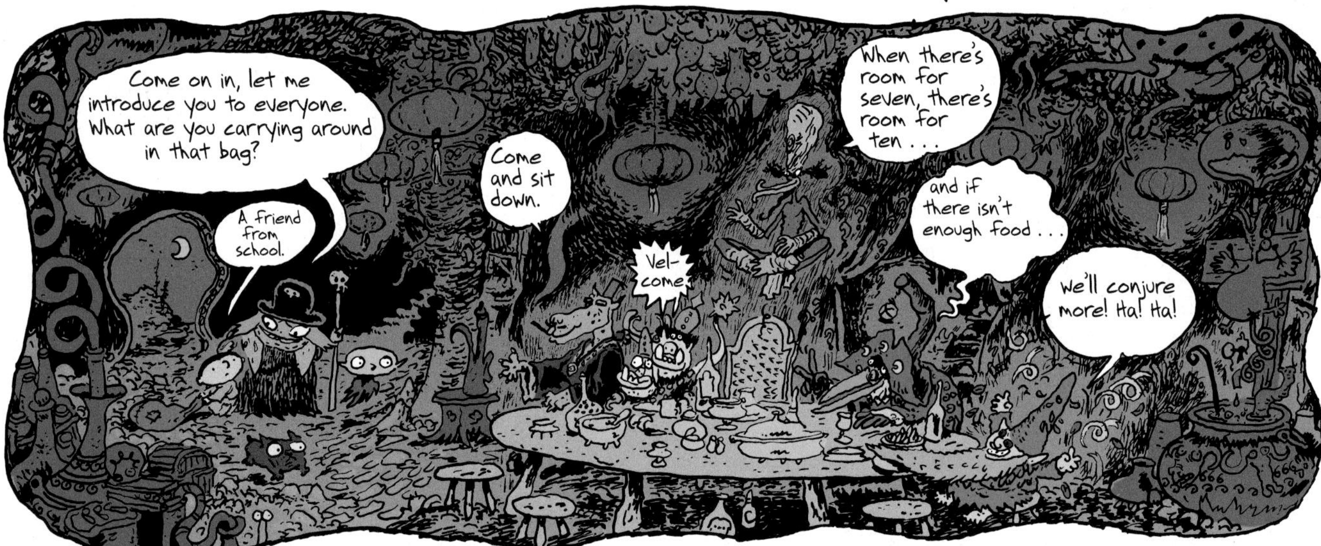
Come on in, let me introduce you to everyone. What are you carrying around in that bag?
A friend from school.
Come and sit down.
Vel-come.
When there's room for seven, there's room for ten . . .
and if there isn't enough food . . .
We'll conjure more! Ha! Ha!

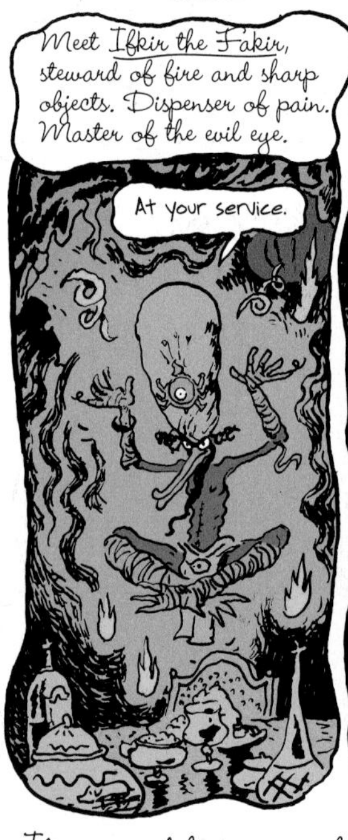
Meet Ifkir the Fakir, steward of fire and sharp objects. Dispenser of pain. Master of the evil eye.
At your service.

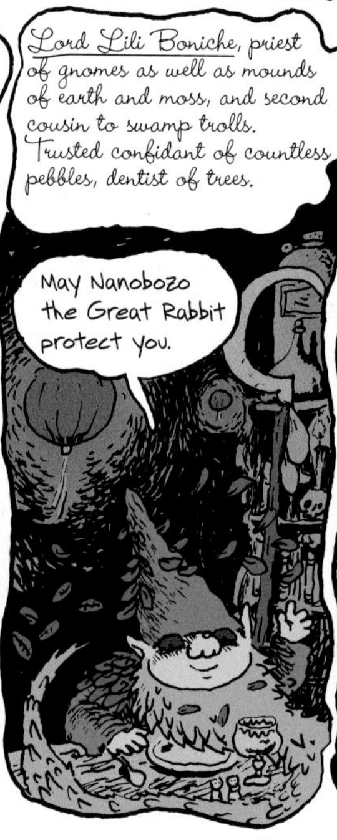
Lord Lili Boniche, priest of gnomes as well as mounds of earth and moss, and second cousin to swamp trolls. Trusted confidant of countless pebbles, dentist of trees.
May Nanobozo the Great Rabbit protect you.

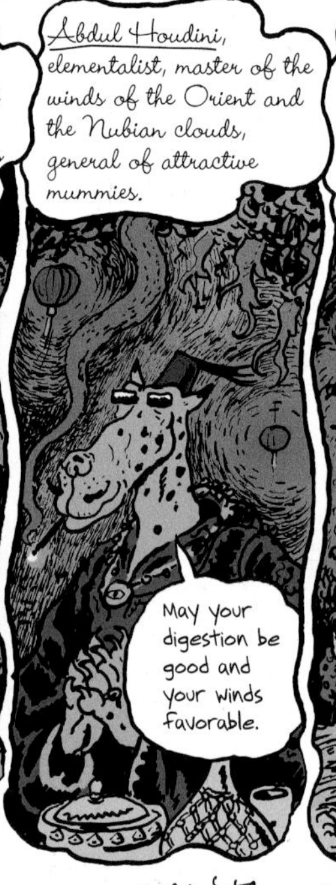
Abdul Houdini, elementalist, master of the winds of the Orient and the Nubian clouds, general of attractive mummies.
May your digestion be good and your winds favorable.

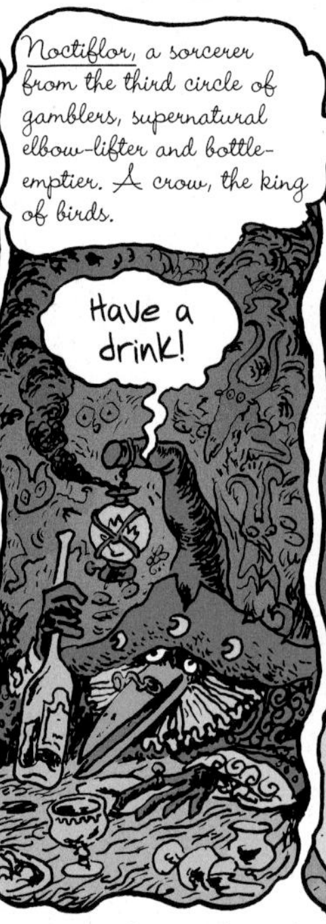
Noctiflor, a sorcerer from the third circle of gamblers, supernatural elbow-lifter and bottle-emptier. A crow, the king of birds.
Have a drink!

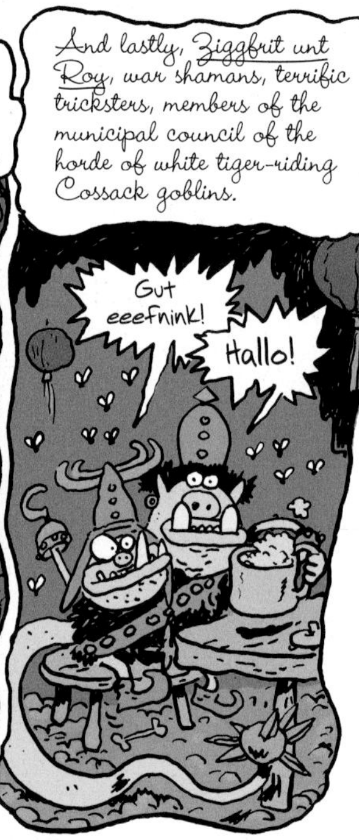
And lastly, Ziggfrit unt Roy, war shamans, terrific tricksters, members of the municipal council of the horde of white tiger-riding Cossack goblins.
Gut eeefnink!
Hallo!

It was a delicious meal, and many incredible stories were told. They ate cakes from the other end of the world, some of which cracked and wriggled in your mouth as though they were full of small insects, but they were tasty . . .

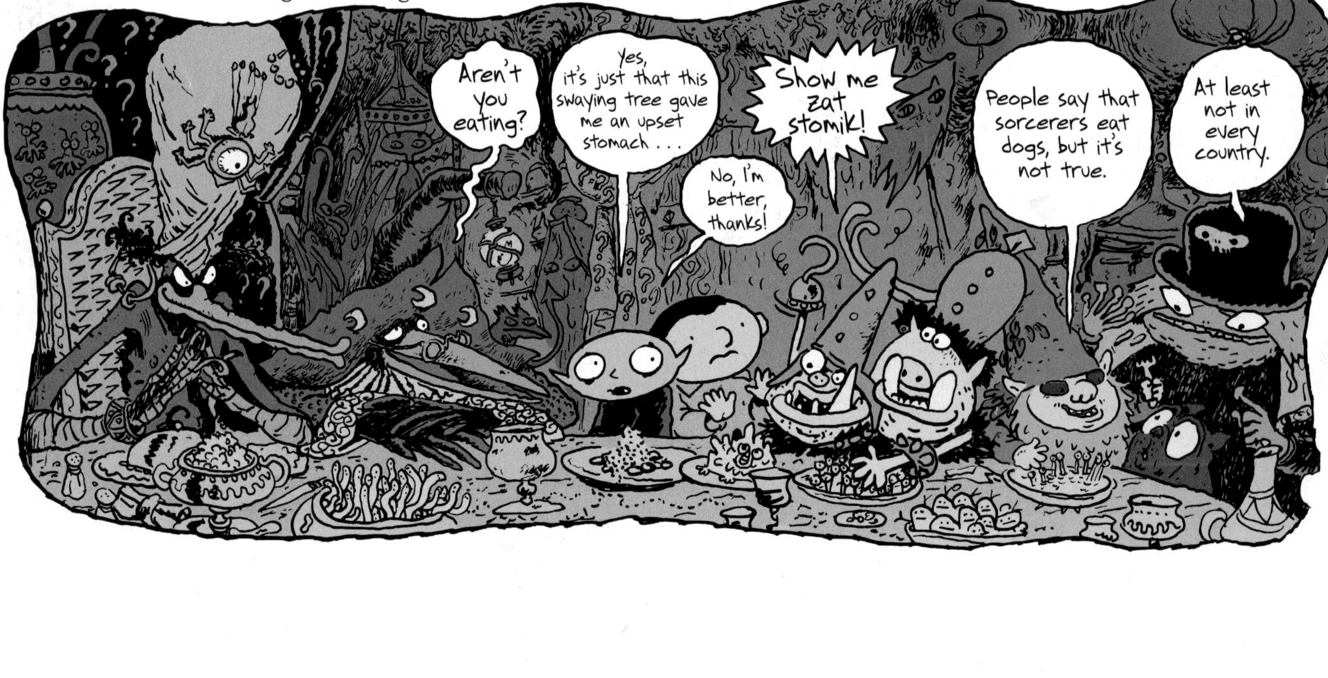
Aren't you eating?
Yes, it's just that this swaying tree gave me an upset stomach . . .
No, I'm better, thanks!
Show me zat stomik!
People say that sorcerers eat dogs, but it's not true.
At least not in every country.

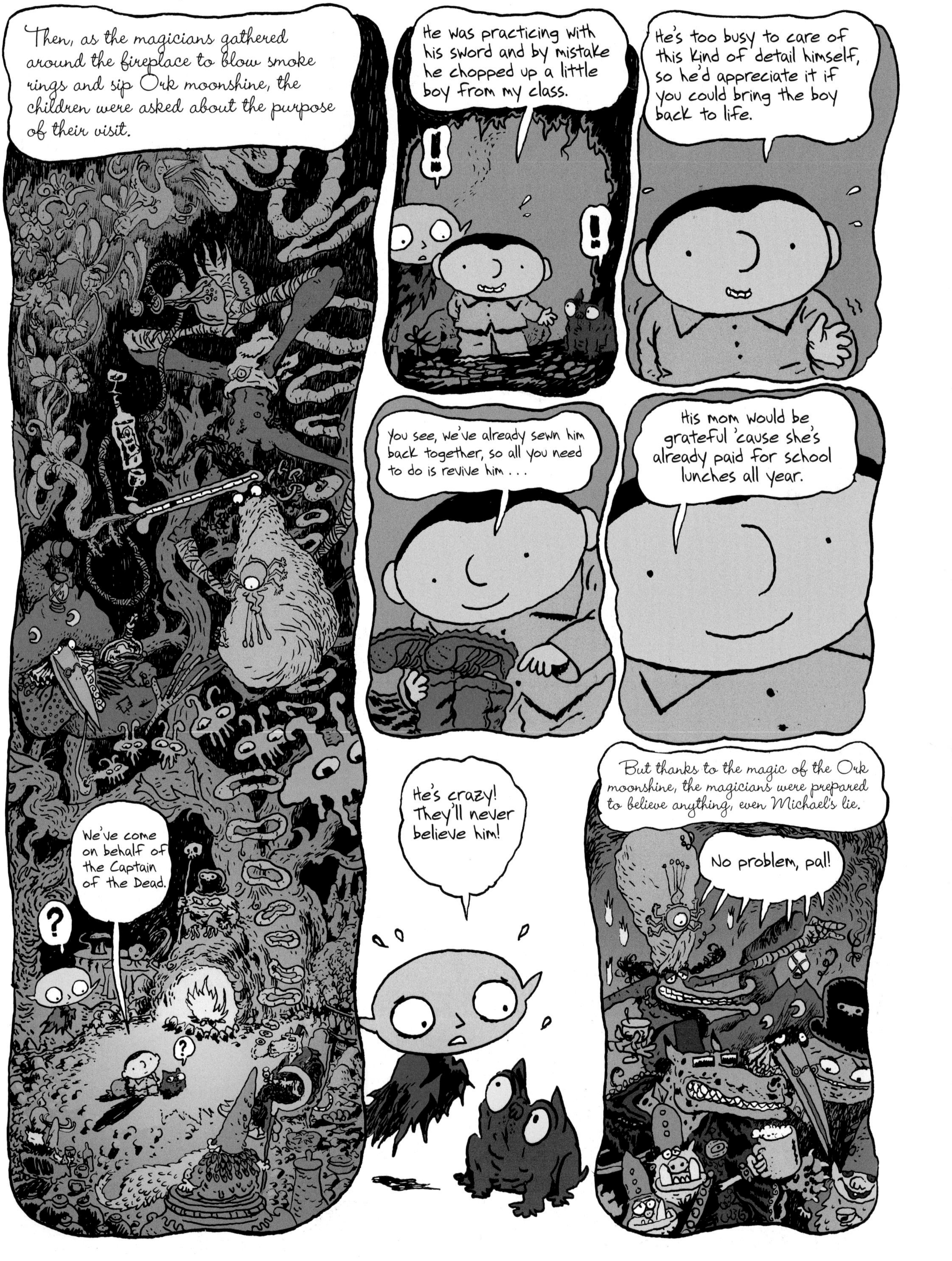
Then, as the magicians gathered around the fireplace to blow smoke rings and sip Ork moonshine, the children were asked about the purpose of their visit.
We've come on behalf of the Captain of the Dead.
?
?
He was practicing with his sword and by mistake he chopped up a little boy from my class.
!
!
He's too busy to care of this kind of detail himself, so he'd appreciate it if you could bring the boy back to life.
You see, we've already sewn him back together, so all you need to do is revive him . . .
His mom would be grateful 'cause she's already paid for school lunches all year.
He's crazy! They'll never believe him!
But thanks to the magic of the Ork moonshine, the magicians were prepared to believe anything, even Michael's lie.
No problem, pal!

Then each magician explained how he would go about reviving Jeffrey if Michael entrusted him with the job.

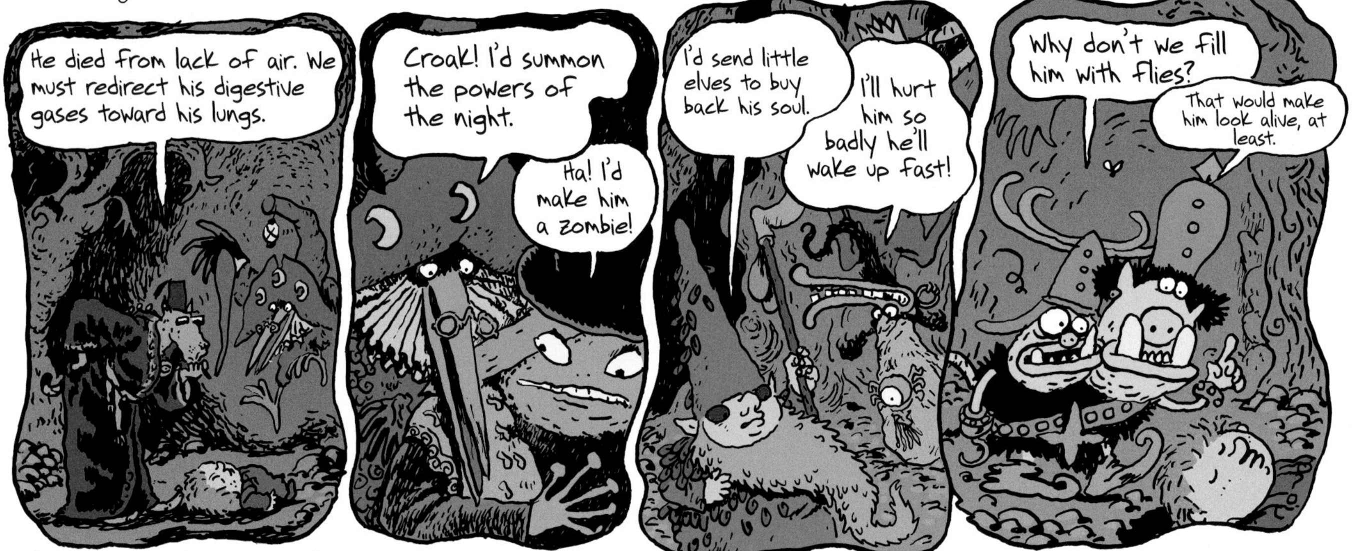
He died from lack of air. We must redirect his digestive gases toward his lungs.
Croak! I'd summon the powers of the night.
Ha! I'd make him a zombie!
I'd send little elves to buy back his soul.
I'll hurt him so badly he'll wake up fast!
Why don't we fill him with flies?
That would make him look alive, at least.

Neither Michael, nor Little Vampire, nor Phantomat understood a thing the experts said. They didn't know whom to choose.

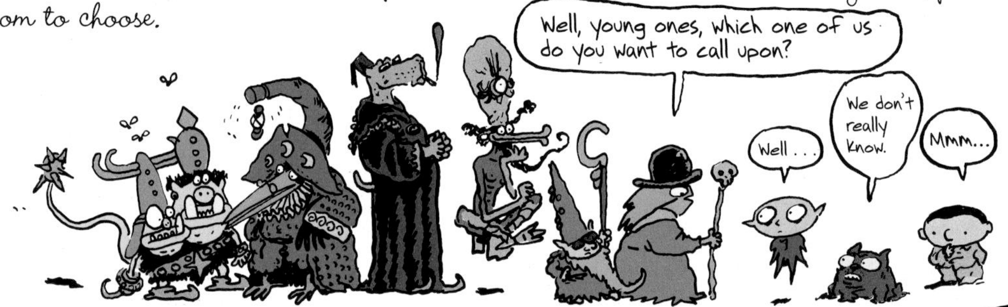
Well, young ones, which one of us do you want to call upon?
Well . . .
We don't really know.
Mmm...

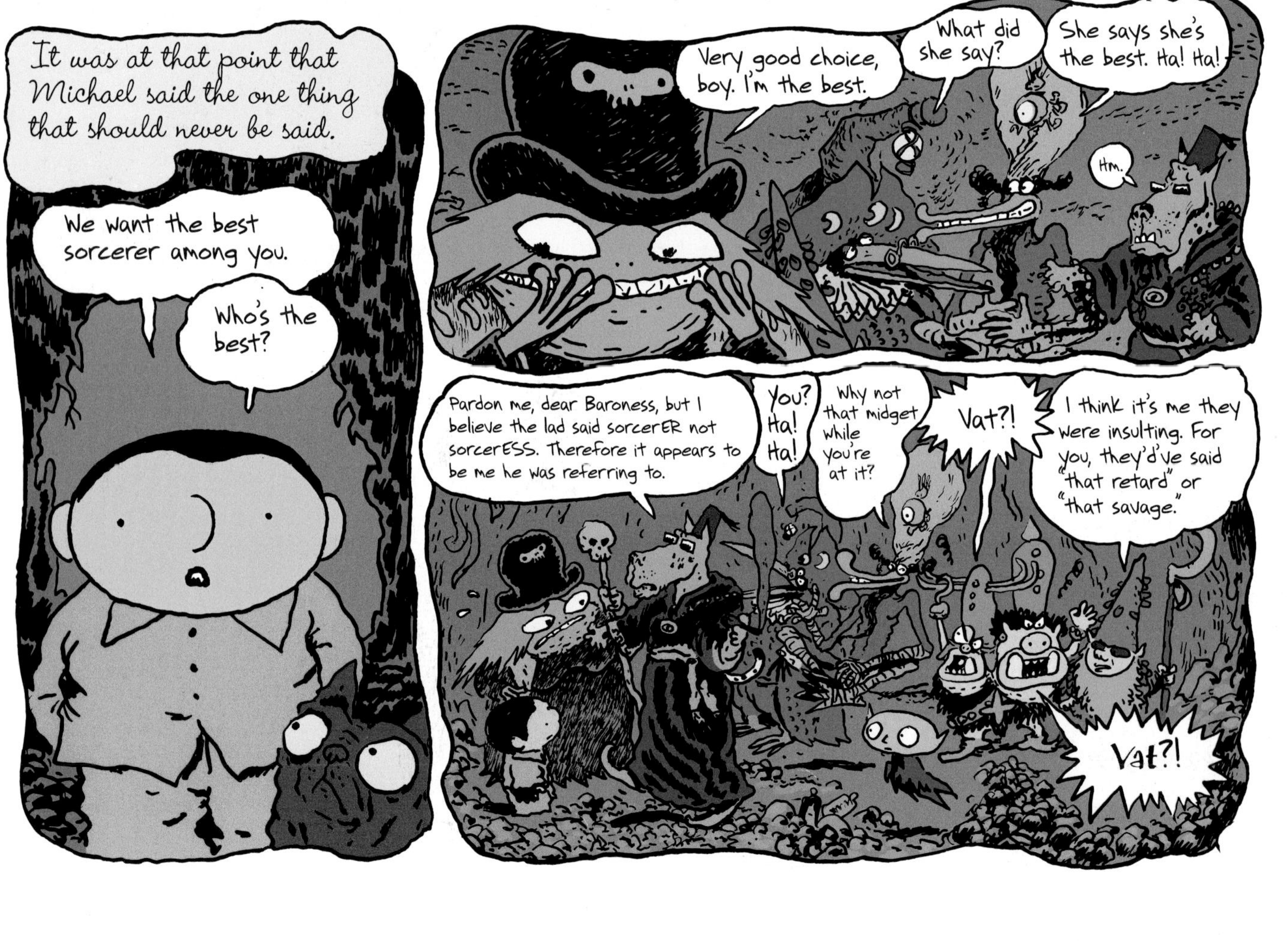
It was at that point that Michael said the one thing that should never be said.
We want the best sorcerer among you.
Who's the best?
Very good choice, boy. I'm the best.
What did she say?
She says she's the best. Ha! Ha!
Hm.
Pardon me, dear Baroness, but I believe the lad said sorcerER not sorcerESS. Therefore it appears to be me he was referring to.
You? Ha! Ha!
Why not that midget while you're at it?
Vat?!
I think it's me they were insulting. For you, they'd've said "that retard" or "that savage."
Vat?!

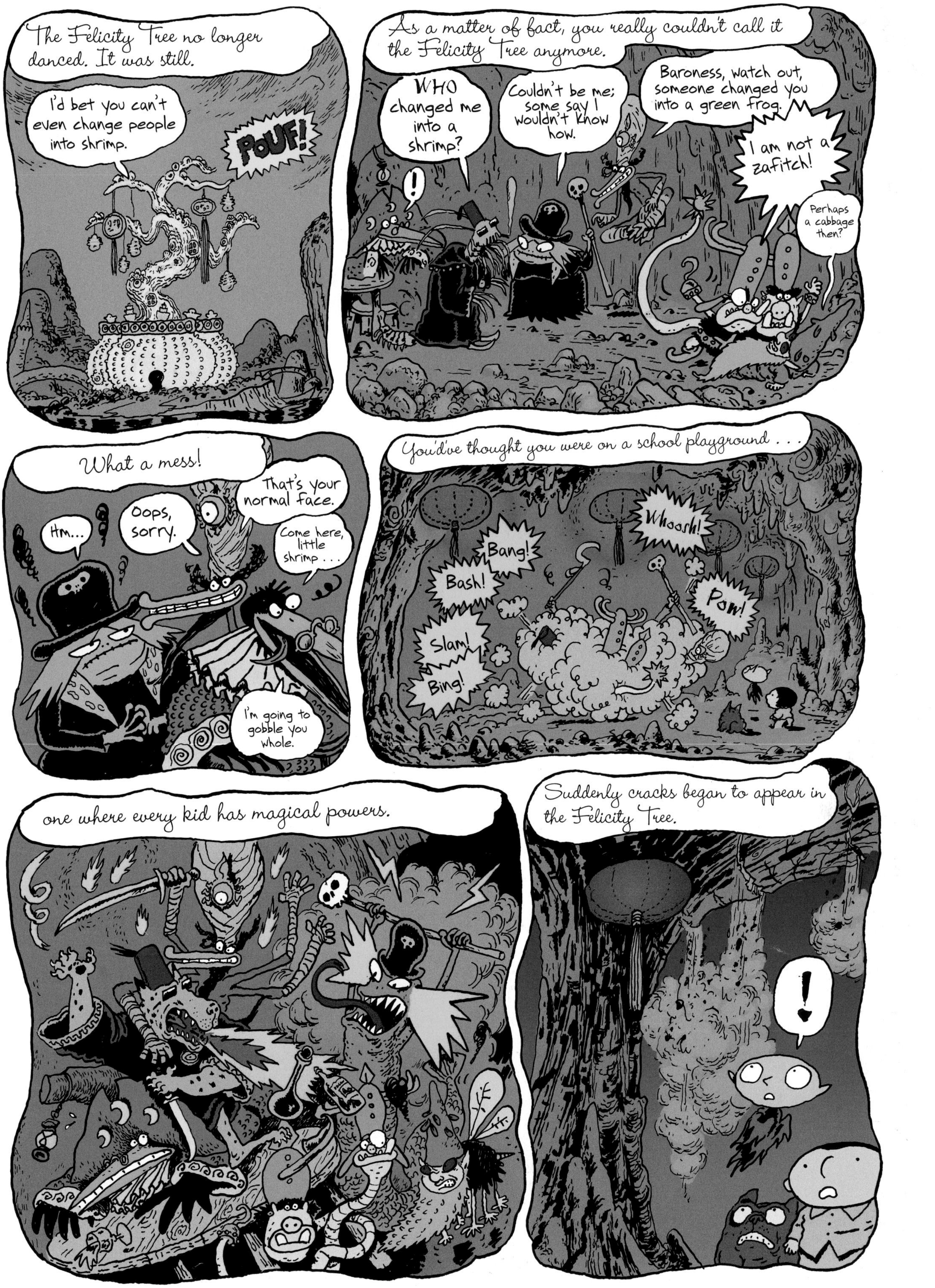
The Felicity Tree no longer danced. It was still.
I'd bet you can't even change people into shrimp.
POUF!
As a matter of fact, you really couldn't call it the Felicity Tree anymore.
WHO changed me into a shrimp?
!
Couldn't be me; some say I wouldn't know how.
Baroness, watch out, someone changed you into a green frog.
I am not a zafitch!
Perhaps a cabbage then?
What a mess!
Hm...
Oops, sorry.
That's your normal face.
Come here, little shrimp . . .
I'm going to gobble you whole.
You'd've thought you were on a school playground . . .
Whoosh!
Bang!
Bash!
Pow!
Slam!
Bing!
one where every kid has magical powers.
Suddenly cracks began to appear in the Felicity Tree.
!

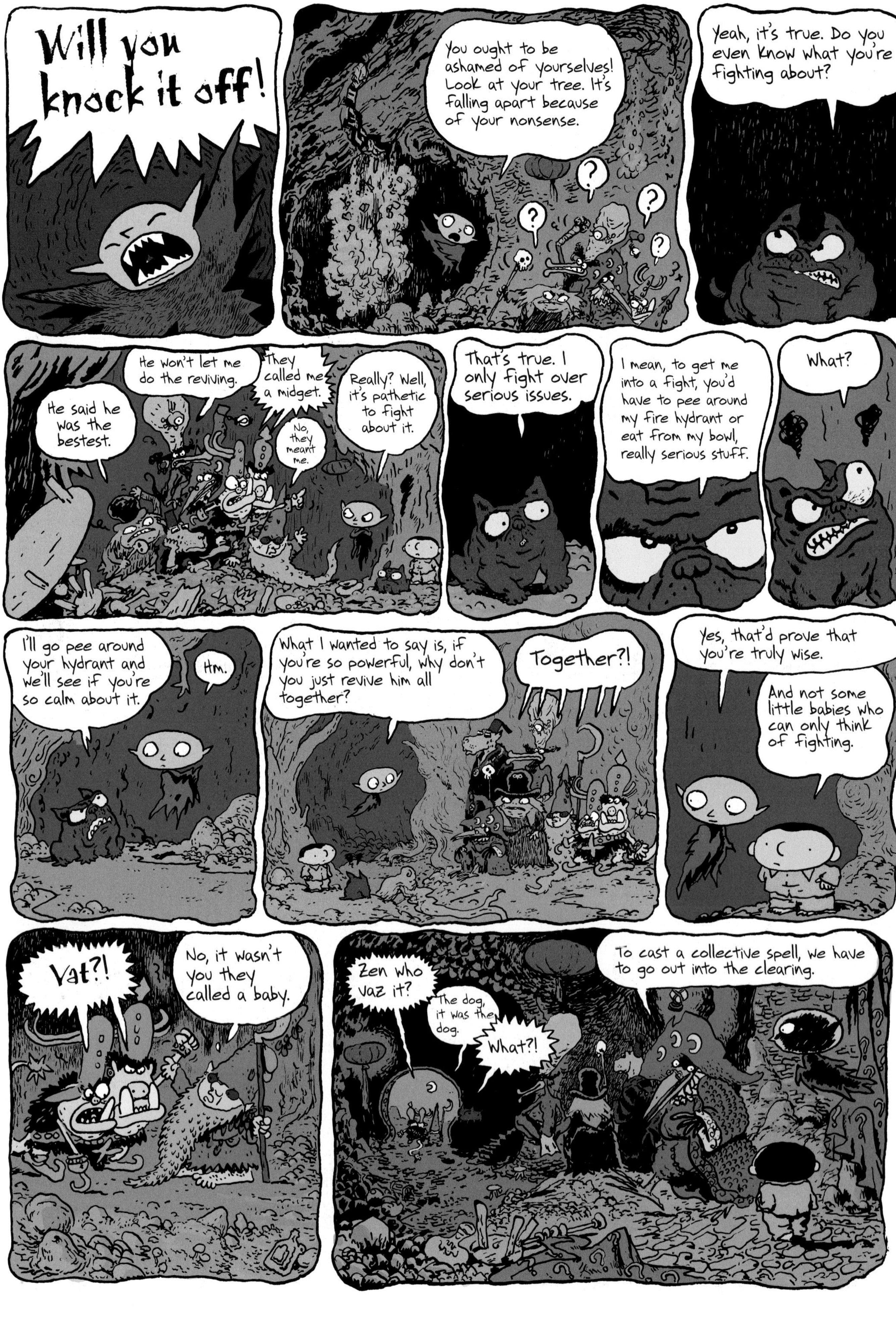
Will you knock it off!
You ought to be ashamed of yourselves! Look at your tree. It's falling apart because of your nonsense.
?
?
?
?
Yeah, it's true. Do you even know what you're fighting about?
He said he was the bestest.
He won't let me do the reviving.
They called me a midget.
No, they meant me.
Really? Well, it's pathetic to fight about it.
That's true. I only fight over serious issues.
I mean, to get me into a fight, you'd have to pee around my fire hydrant or eat from my bowl, really serious stuff.
What?
I'll go pee around your hydrant and we'll see if you're so calm about it.
Hm.
What I wanted to say is, if you're so powerful, why don't you just revive him all together?
Together?!
Yes, that'd prove that you're truly wise.
And not some little babies who can only think of fighting.
Vat?!
No, it wasn't you they called a baby.
Zen who vaz it?
The dog, it was the dog.
What?!
To cast a collective spell, we have to go out into the clearing.

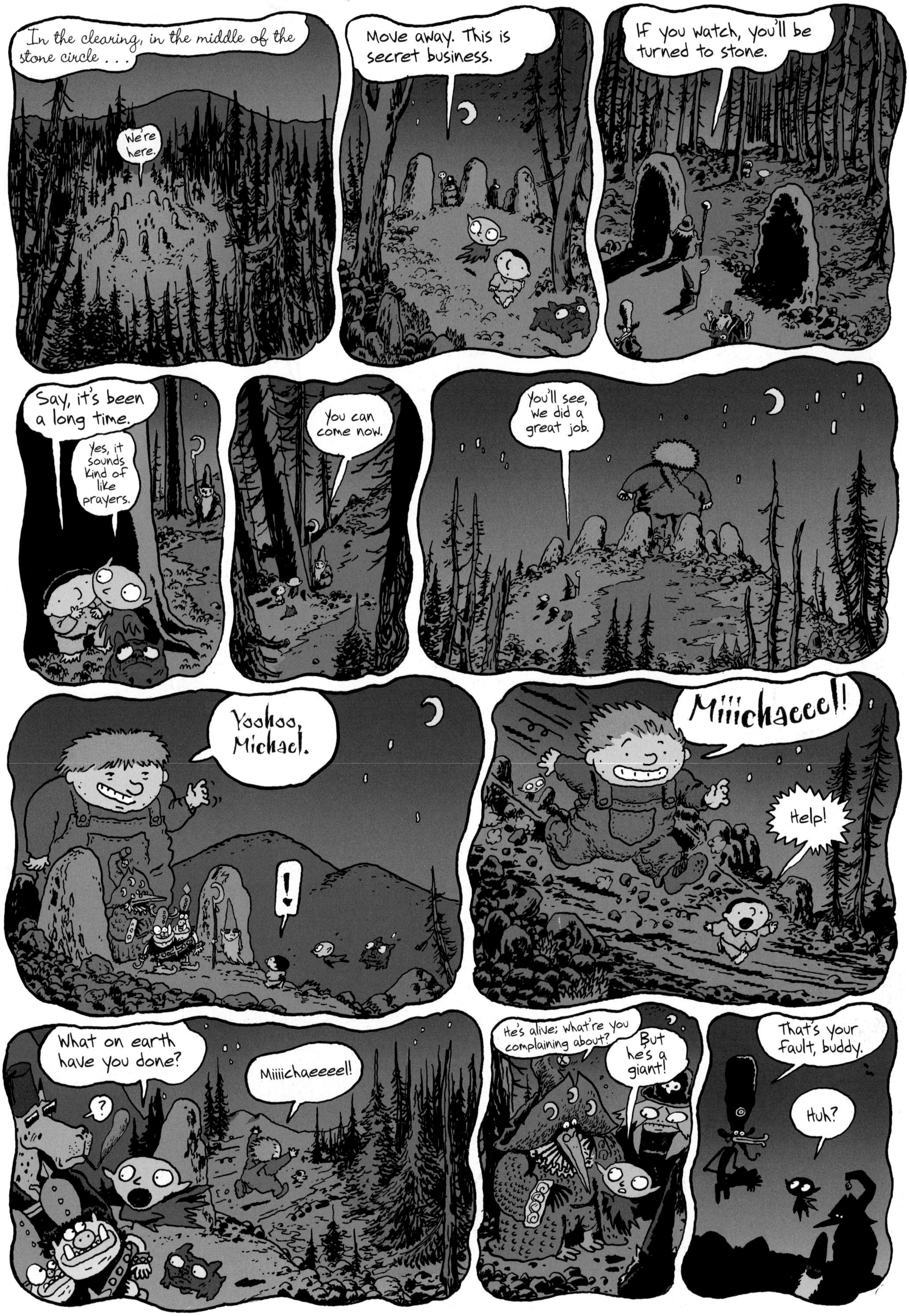
In the clearing, in the middle of the stone circle . . .
We're here.
Move away. This is secret business.
If you watch, you'll be turned to stone.
Say, it's been a long time.
Yes, it sounds kind of like prayers.
You can come now.
You'll see, we did a great job.
Yoohoo, Michael.
!
Miiichaeeel!
Help!
What on earth have you done?
?
Miiichaeeeel!
He's alive; what're you complaining about?
But he's a giant!
That's your fault, buddy.
Huh?

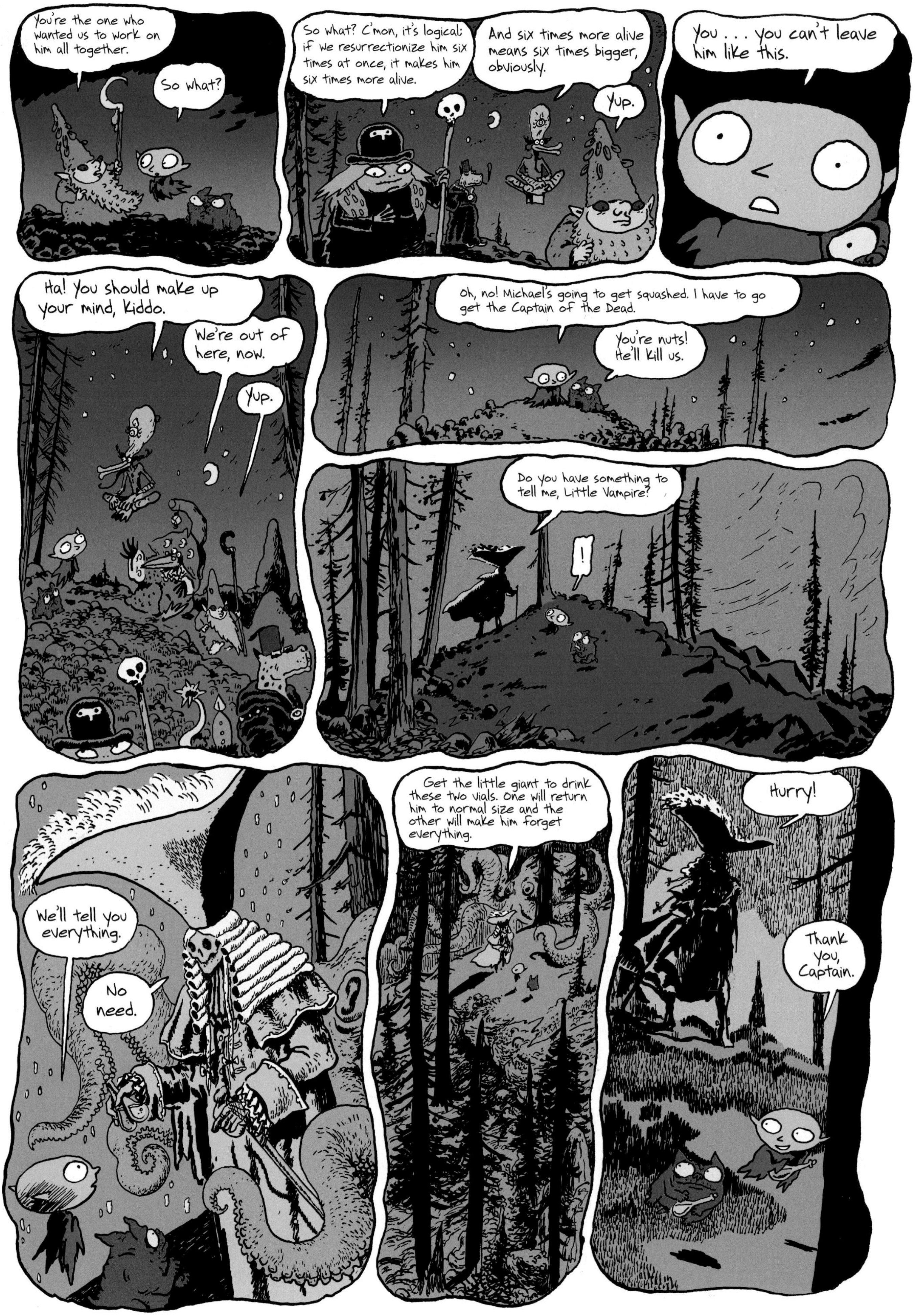

You're the one who wanted us to work on him all together.
So what?
So what? C'mon, it's logical; if we resurrectionize him six times at once, it makes him six times more alive.
And six times more alive means six times bigger, obviously.
Yup.
You . . . you can't leave him like this.
Ha! You should make up your mind, kiddo.
We're out of here, now.
Yup.
Oh, no! Michael's going to get squashed. I have to go get the Captain of the Dead.
You're nuts! He'll kill us.
Do you have something to tell me, Little Vampire?
!
We'll tell you everything.
No need.
Get the little giant to drink these two vials. One will return him to normal size and the other will make him forget everything.
Hurry!
Thank you, Captain.

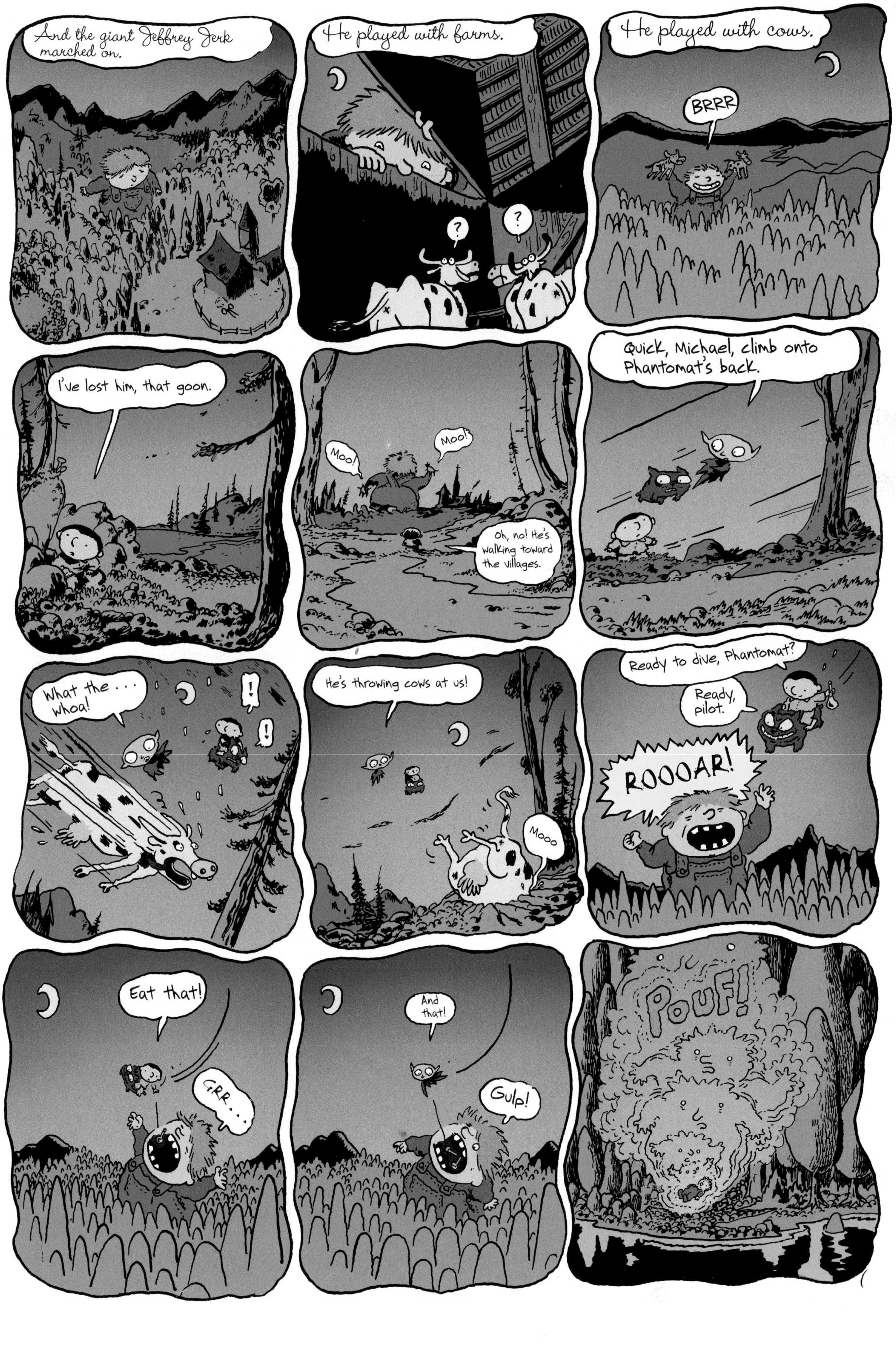
And the giant Jeffrey Jerk marched on.
He played with farms.
?
?
He played with cows.
BRRR
I've lost him, that goon.
Moo!
Moo!
Oh, no! He's walking toward the villages.
Quick, Michael, climb onto Phantomat's back.
What the . . . whoa!
!
!
He's throwing cows at us!
Mooo
Ready to dive, Phantomat?
Ready, pilot.
ROOOAR!
Eat that!
GRR . . .
And that!
Gulp!
POUF!

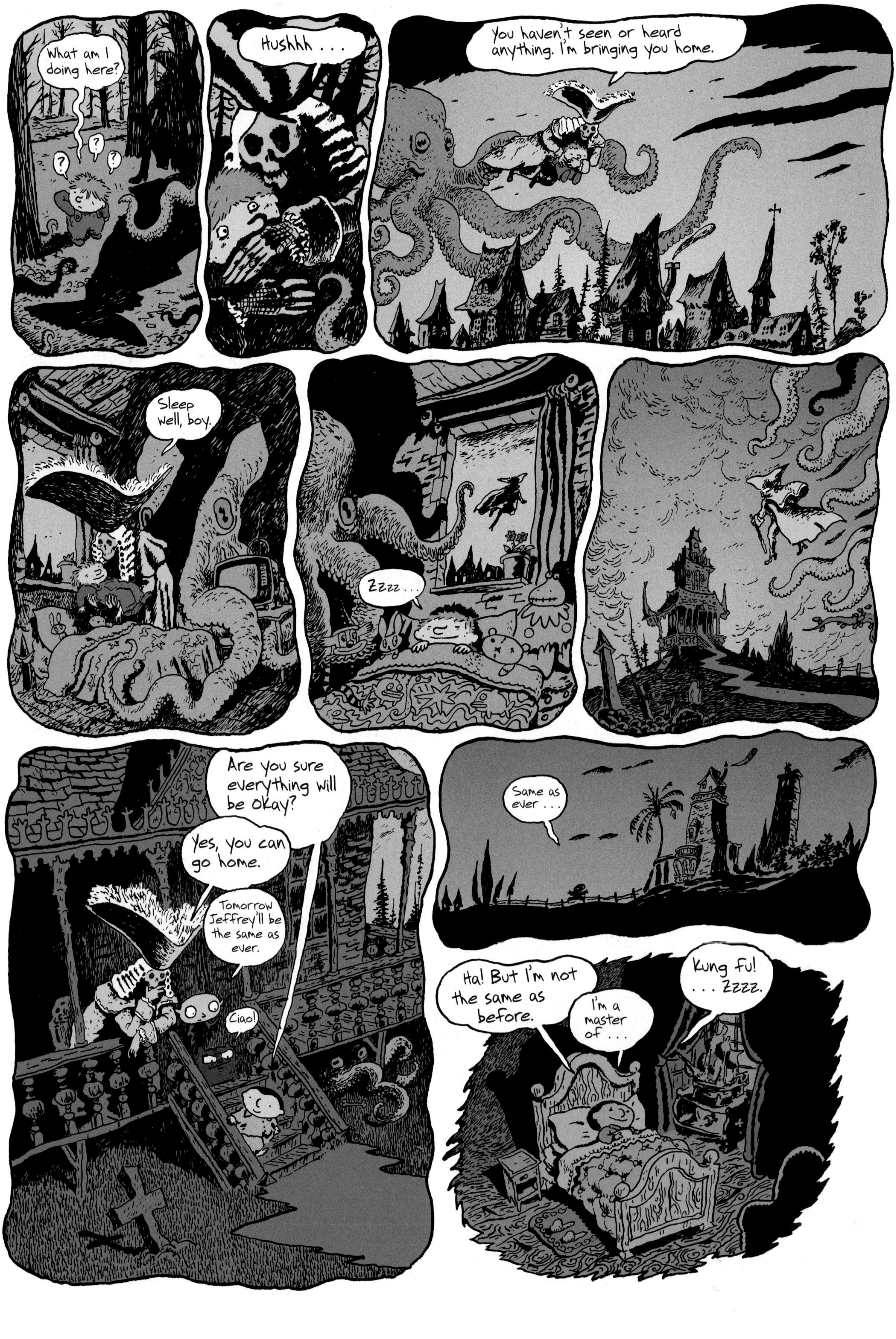
What am I doing here?
?
?
?
Hushhh . . .
You haven't seen or heard anything. I'm bringing you home.
Sleep well, boy.
Zzzz . . .
Are you sure everything will be okay?
Yes, you can go home.
Tomorrow Jeffrey'll be the same as ever.
Ciao!
Same as ever . . .
Ha! But I'm not the same as before.
I'm a master of . . .
Kung fu! . . . Zzzz.

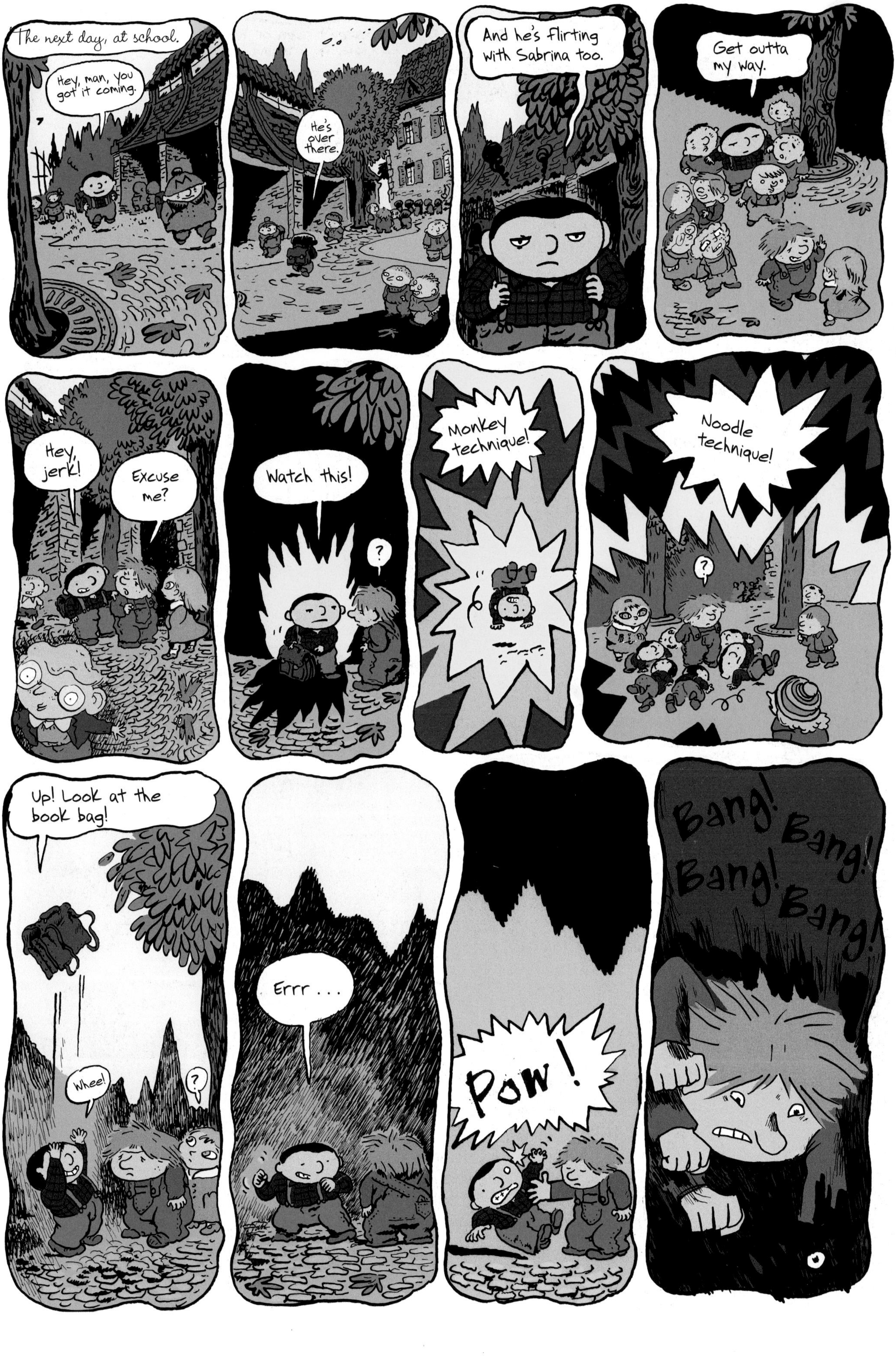
The next day, at school.
Hey, man, you got it coming.
He's over there.
And he's flirting with Sabrina too.
Get outta my way.
Hey, jerk!
Excuse me?
Watch this!
?
Monkey technique!
Noodle technique!
?
Up! Look at the book bag!
Whee!
?
Errr . . .
POW!
Bang! Bang! Bang! Bang!

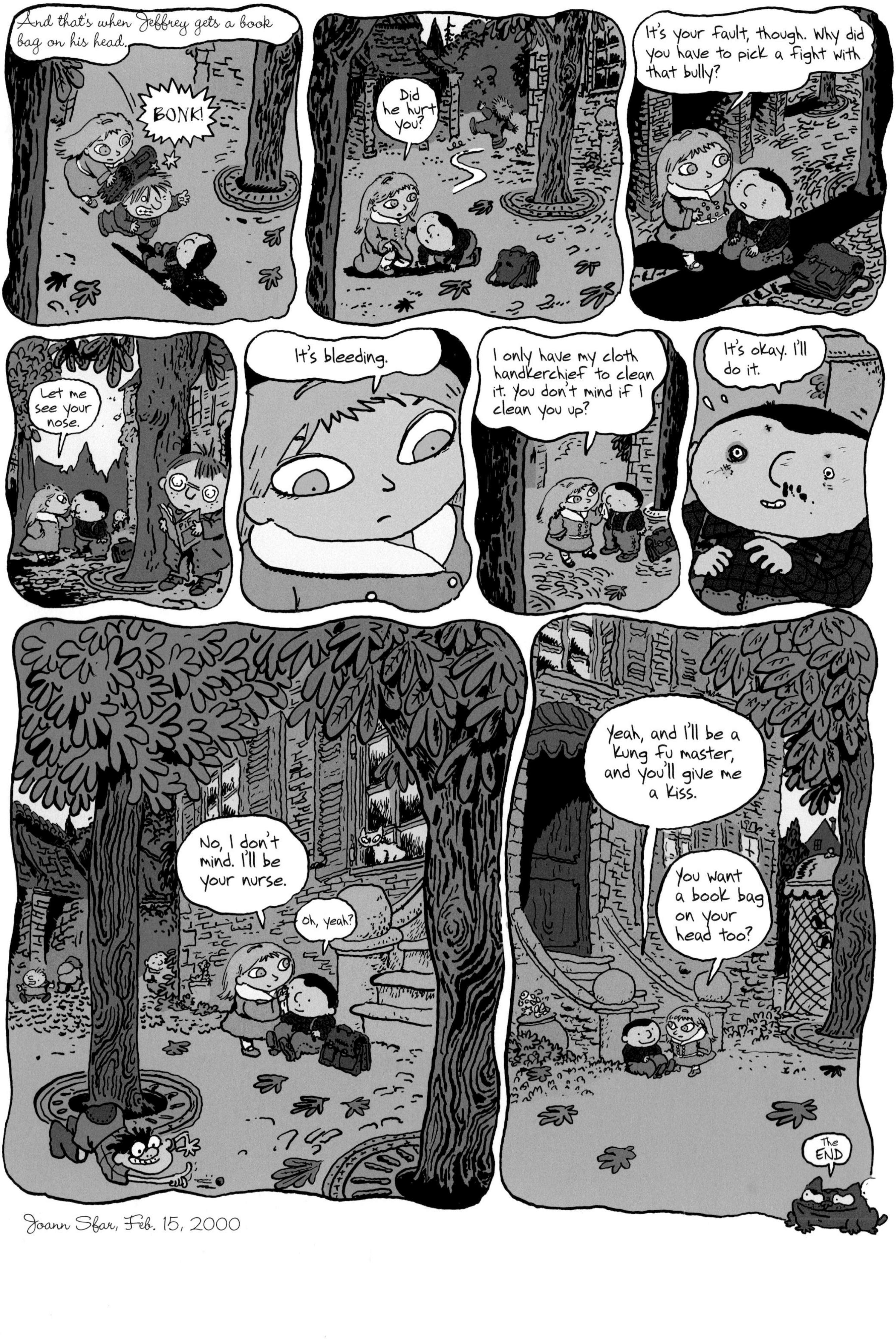
And that's when Jeffrey gets a book bag on his head.
BONK!
Did he hurt you?
It's your fault, though. Why did you have to pick a fight with that bully?
Let me see your nose.
It's bleeding.
I only have my cloth handkerchief to clean it. You don't mind if I clean you up?
It's okay. I'll do it.
No, I don't mind. I'll be your nurse.
Oh, yeah?
Yeah, and I'll be a kung fu master, and you'll give me a kiss.
You want a book bag on your head too?
The END

Joann Sfar, Feb. 15, 2000

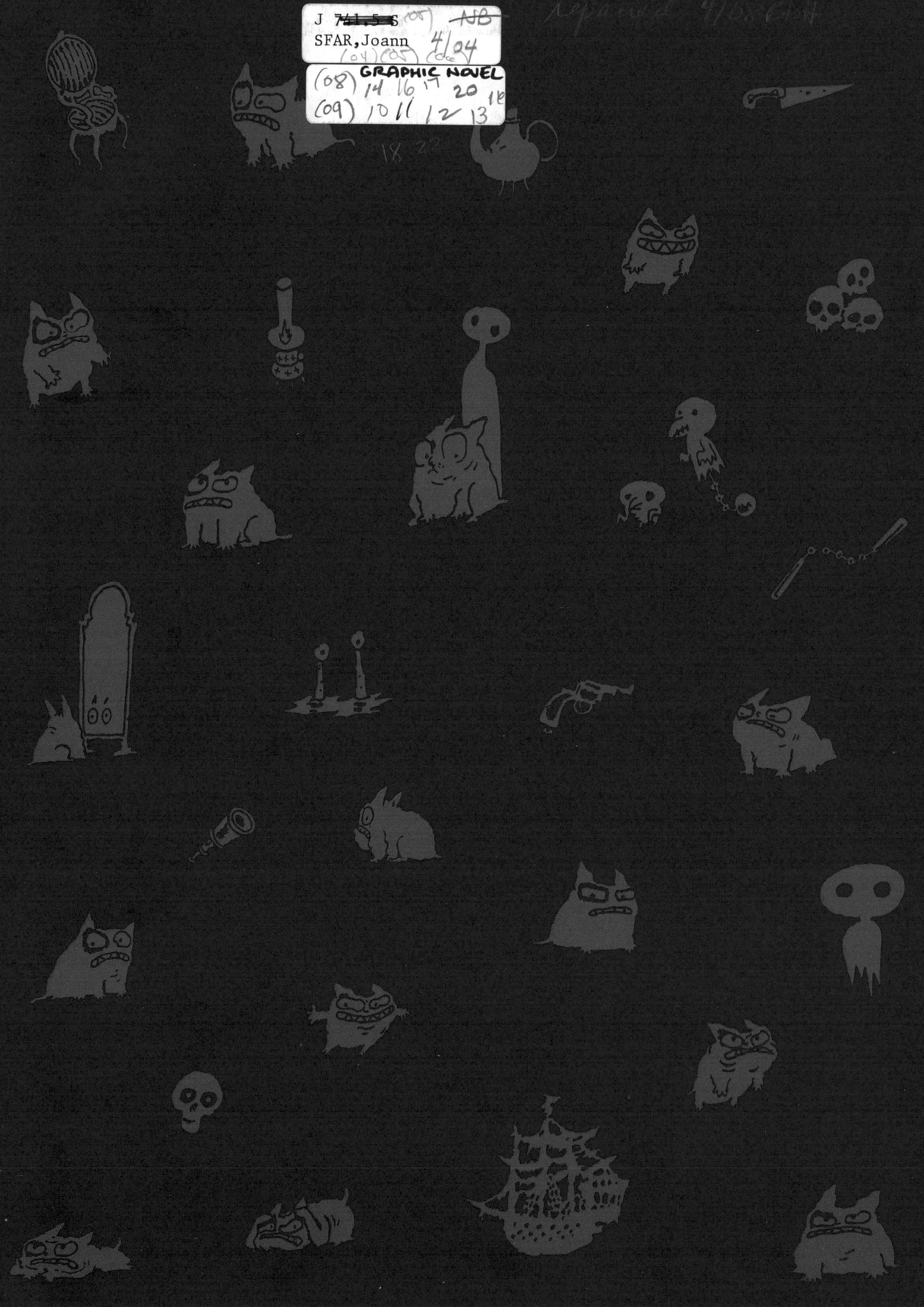